# 10

Russ Crossley

Published by 53rd Street Publishing

# Table of Contents

*A deadly battle on the moon…*

A flash of a laser beam shot across the no mans land from one of the enemy bots. It struck Dr. Helen Tasker's TIN Man and sliced her torso in two. It was almost as if her shields weren't on.

"Will." It was Holly. "I've picked up a low frequency wave that's interfering with our shield generators." She paused and the information sunk in. If the enemy was able to do this then maybe all of their systems could be compromised.

"Helen!" Will called.

"Yes," Helen said her voice trembling with fear.

"Check your generator power level."

There was a short pause then she replied, "It's reading zero. And it's not related to the damage I've sustained."

Now Will was worried.

# Introduction

I'm very pleased to offer you a ten-story collection of my science fiction and fantasy stories. I've been a fan of science fiction since I was a child watching the Mercury, Gemini, and Apollo space programs in the 1960's. I began, like most children, reading comic books mostly related to science fiction.

Super heroes, UFO's, aliens, anything that smacked of science fiction or fantasy I would read it. And any movie or television show with science fiction or fantasy elements were my staple of entertainment viewing, and believe me the special effects weren't what they are today.

What was common about science fiction and fantasy stories then was the stories often had uplifting endings and the good guys won. They always won. Or if they didn't win the story told how they survived their terrible circumstances. Don't misunderstand me I really love science fiction today, even without endings where the hero clearly wins.

I hope you enjoy this collection of my stories and hope they will become your favorites.

In the science fiction section of this collection you will find stories with impossible odds, satire where the fast food companies run the future, AI robots locked in a civil war, and space travelers with very human problems.

In the fantasy section are stories of alternate realities, a vampire castaway, dragons, cheerleaders, and a man asked to fix a UFO. It's quite a collection and diverse enough for most readers of fantastic fiction to enjoy.

Feel free to contact me on twitter or facebook. I'd love to hear from you.

Enjoy!
Russ Crossley
April 2013

# 10

Russ Crossley

Published by 53rd Street Publishing

ISBN 978-1-927621-14-1

Cover image © Angela Harburn | Dreamstime.com

This is a work of fiction. The persons and situations are products of the authors imagination,

Logo image by:

Engraver | Dreamstime.com

# Countdown

ELVIS PEPPER SAT ON HIS BUNK staring at the image on the monitor on his desk. His eyes brimmed with tears and his mind was having trouble processing what he was seeing.

When the asteroid the size of Texas struck the Earth in the Atlantic Ocean it vaporized that ocean and hurled a huge cloud of dust and debris high into the atmosphere. The clouds of superheated air quickly formed a shroud around the Earth and winds spread a wave of destruction at speeds of over two hundred and fifty miles an hour outward in waves from the epicenter where the asteroid struck.

The surveillance satellite watching the catastrophe was stationed within range of the electromagnetic pulse so as expected within a few minutes of impact the satellite's transmission feed was lost.

As the screen changed to white fuzz a tear escaped Elvis' right eye and traveled down his cheek. In the next few hours everything humanity had built over the last ten thousand years would be scoured from the surface of the planet by a force greater than the collective power of every atomic weapon ever constructed. Nature had provided a far more lethal end for the Earth than mankind ever could.

The four orbiting Lagrange stations in Earth orbit, and the fifth at L2 position on the other side of the moon, would keep the dream of humanity alive. All that remained now of the human race were twenty thousand Adam and Eve's to start over, and hopefully some day re-populate the Earth.

Like a zombie Elvis got up from his bunk and walked to the desk where he fingered the off button on the side of the monitor and it went dark. He let out a slow breath. He'd been preparing for this day for five years yet when the time came the image of such terrible destruction affected him at a far deeper level than he had anticipated.

After he wiped his eyes with the back of his hand he went to the door of his cabin and keyed the code into the keypad set in the wall next to the door. After a barely audible click the door slide aside and he stepped into the corridor.

He passed several cabin doors on his way to the communication center where he was due to relieve Selma Hollings. It had been two hours since impact and they were supposed to keep monitoring communications from the underground bunkers where Earth bound survivors were housed, as were the other L stations.

The bunkers were constructed in the twentieth century during the cold war. Now in the middle of the twenty-first century the bunkers were being used to protect a cadre of scientists and other experts that were unsuccessful in the world wide lottery for the twenty thousand coveted positions on the Lagrangian stations, or those deemed ineligible for the lottery due to age or for medical reasons but were still valuable.

Only fertile people between the ages of twelve and forty-five were eligible to enter the lottery, but the worlds leading scientists agreed these bunkers would save an additional thirty thousand people. They expected these survivors would be able to hold out in the bunkers for the next five years. Estimates were the dust and debris thrown into the atmosphere would have settled by then.

But Elvis wasn't worried about the survival of thirty thousand people. He was concerned about the survival of one person. His wife, Yvette.

Her PhD in immunization technology made her eligible for the bunker in the Ural Mountains after she was deemed unsuitable for the lottery. Her inability to have children made her ineligible to even apply. But her scientific expertise made her indispensable for the future survival in the harsh environment expected in five years.

He told her wouldn't go without her, but he would never have qualified for one of the bunkers. After many long, tearful arguments he agreed to go to the L1 station. They would stay linked by com sat as long as they were able. They would both survive just not together.

Now that he'd witnessed the destruction he knew he'd made the wrong decision.

I should have stayed with her as long as possible, he thought. But then I'd be dead.

A lump of fear knotted his guts and his heart beat hard in his chest. He grew more anxious with each step as he raced to the communications center. He was one of five specialists responsible to maintain and operate the com systems between the stations. And for the time being with any Earth based survivors.

The stations were shielded against electromagnetic interference so unlike the satellites they would be able to maintain communications.

"I need to stay focused," he muttered as he passed cabin after cabin. The sobs of his fellow survivors echoed in the empty corridor and followed him as he rushed toward the lift that would take him to the command deck. The captain would need him today so he had to shake off his fear and his uncertainty.

Problem was he wasn't sure he could put aside what remained of his humanity. In fact he wasn't sure any of them could.

The lift doors closed behind him after he entered. Good thing he was alone because he wanted to scream out how unfair all this was. He closed his eyes and sighed.

The end of the world, the separation from his wife, the end of everything he held dear felt like a tremendous weight crushing him under waves of despair.

He would never feel a warm breeze on his face, or witness the sunrise over the purple mountains at his late father's cabin on Seesaw Mountain. He'd never swim in the ocean or smell wood smoke from a campfire. Stars would never twinkle again and his dog would never run in the tall grass behind his uncle's barn.

The doors opened as the lift stopped on the command deck.

He opened his eyes and stepped out just before the doors closed behind him.

No one was around. He was alone. Walking to the com panel he touched the power button. The board lit up and the screens came to life. Even though the station was shielded the captain ordered all nonessential systems be powered down until after impact.

The screens flickered then steadied. The external cameras directed at Earth showed the fierce red cloud of explosive energy had spread half way across the United States laying waste to cities, towns, open plains, everything. Every plant, animal, and human would be vaporized. No pain, no suffering.

In a way he almost envied them. At least their end would be quick. If the eggheads were correct the debris trailing the asteroid might end this attempt at keeping the human race viable even before it began again. A rocky missile the size of a tennis ball would puncture the station and compromise its atmosphere killing most if not all of the inhabitants in the process.

Elvis felt smaller and more insignificant than he had ever in his life. "Activate holo-assistant," he said as he picked up a com node and placed it in his right ear.

There was a shimmer and Maple appeared next to him.

She wore a sad-eyed, sympathetic expression on her holographic features. Dressed in her lab suit with her glasses perched on the end of her small nose she looked every part the scientist the designer had built into her.

Though Elvis knew her emotions were memory engrams programmed into her matrix he really needed a friend right now. Since Maple had been with him since his training started five years ago she had become a friend. He smiled to himself as he recalled the memory of Yvette actually getting jealous of the "other woman" in his life.

"Good times," he said quietly.

"I disagree," said Maple in a dulcet tone.

Elvis paused to look at her. "What?"

"Well, sir, this is not a *good time*, as you put it. It is the end of planet Earth as a home for humans."

"Thanks for reminding me," he said sarcastically. He shook his head. "I was recalling one happy memory and you had to ruin it."

Maple's eyes widened. "Sorry, sir. Sometimes I forget my manners."

"Never mind. Contact L3 and see if they can get me an angle of the bunker in the Ural Mountains. Or is that too difficult?"

"No, sir, right away."

After a short pause a familiar voice came through the com node in his ear. "L3, Pumper Jackson speaking."

"Pump, it's E. I need a link to your cams directed at the Ural bunkers."

"Hey, E. Man, wasn't that impact thingy sumthin?"

"Yeah, Pump, it was that." His heart skipped a beat and for a second he thought his next words would catch in his throat. He coughed then managed to say, "Anyway, can you set up the link?"

"Isn't that where Yvette is?"

'Yeah, Pump she's there. And will you boost the signal for me so I can talk to her?"

"I need authorization from—"

"Really, Pump? Really?! It's me, Pump!" He tried to control the anger in his voice but failed. He didn't need a lecture on procedure right now. He needed to talk to his wife before it was too late.

Elvis sighed heavily and his shoulders slumped. "Sorry, Pump. I didn't mean to be short with you. It's just that—" His next words caught at the back of his throat.

"Yeah, okay, E. No problemo. I'll have Lucy establish the link right away." Lucy was Pump's holo-assistant. "Set your monitor to receive."

"It's done, sir," Maple said before he issued the order.

The monitor flickered then steadied and he could see the Ural range untouched, pristine and rugged jutting into the sky.

West of the mountains the edge of the shock wave headed across Europe. It had just wiped away Germany. Millions of people died as he stared at the monitor.

He swallowed hard then said, "L1 to Ural Command, over."

Silence.

"L1 to Ural command," he repeated.

There was a crackle of static then a heavily accented voice responded. "This is Ural Command. Ivan the Terrible speaking. Go ahead L1."

"Ivan!" Elvis smiled to himself. The big man had befriended both he and Yvette during the initial training phase. They had enjoyed dinners and golf games with Ivan and his wife, Simone. Simone won a spot on L2 so Ivan and he had that much in common. "How're things going?"

"EP! How nice to hear your voice, my friend. So far everything is going as planned.

"We lost contact with the Washington bunkers and the ones in Berlin, Helsinki and Ottawa but they told us that would happen. We're anticipating to reestablish contact twelve hours after the impact wave has dissipated." There was a brief pause. "According to current estimates that should be in two days."

Elvis swiveled in his seat to face Maple. He removed the com node from his ear and wrapped it tight in his fist. He motioned for the hologram to lean closer. "How long until the impact wave reaches the Urals?" he whispered.

"Seventeen minutes," she said.

He nodded then placed the node back in his ear and turned back to face the monitor. "Ivan, I need to speak with Yvette. Can you patch me through?"

"Yes, of course."

There was another pause then his wife's voice came over the node. "E?" she said. He could hear the fear in her voice.

Elvis swallowed hard as his mouth dried. "You okay, my love?"

"Yes. So far," came the reply.

"So far?"

"There have been fifteen suicides reported in the past hour."

No! She couldn't.

There was still a chance however small. "How about you?" His voice trembled as he spoke and his heart began to beat faster.

"Don't be concerned, E. Suicide has never been part of my make up."

He heard her swallow and wanted to jump through the com system to wrap her in his arms. "I know, Yvette. It's just up until now this nightmare has been theoretical. The reality is very different. I'm worried what any of us will do."

"Did you see the impact?" she said changing the subject.

"Yes," he whispered. As long as he lived he'd never forget what he'd seen. That terrible image had been burned into his brain permanently.

"The captain has ordered a full briefing in ten minutes," interrupted Maple. "He wants the entire population to meet in the recreation hall."

He looked at Maple and raised both eyebrows. She understood his meaning. They were on a countdown.

"Fourteen minutes," she said softly.

"Advise my section chief I'll be late."

"I don't think—" Elvis silenced the hologram with a glare.

"Yes, sir."

Elvis flushed the sudden burst of anger from his system by rolling his shoulders and expelling a long, deep breath.

"E, are you okay?" asked Yvette.

"Yes, of course. Don't be concerned about me. I'll be right here after the impact wave has passed your bunker. And I'm staying at this post until we reestablish contact. Nothing or no one can budge me. Like I told you when we last saw each other we will never be apart, ever."

"But they could charge you with something. Maybe treason, or worse."

Yvette had always been too sweet for her own good. It was why he loved her so much. But what did any of that matter now? The governments and their laws that had ruled the planet had been swept away like so many dry leaves in the fall. The chance of any of them, or their eventual offspring, surviving was a long shot and they all knew it. Slim as the odds were they had to at least try. The struggle for survival was what made them human.

"Yvette, my darling does any of that matter anymore?"

She laughed half-heartedly. "No, I guess not."

Elvis glanced at Maple. She held up two fingers. Two minutes until contact.

He was running out of time.

"Yvette, I want you to know I don't blame you for us not being able to have children. The lab accident wasn't your fault. I never thought that not for one millisecond."

"It's okay, E," she said. "You're just—" A sudden burst of static in his ear forced him to yank the com node out. He looked at Maple and she nodded and averted her eyes. The wave of superheated air had struck the Ural mountain range knocking out all communications.

His heart racing Elvis stuffed the com node back in his ear as his eyes flitted over the monitors. The one directed at the Urals showed a blistering mass of red, orange and blue clouds engulfing the entire thousand-mile mountain range. He imagined the iron and minerals in those mountains turning to liquid. Peaks thousands of feet high were melting into molten lead.

How anyone would survive the inferno he didn't know, but his wife had to survive. She just had to.

"Sir?" said Maple from behind him.

"Yes, Maple, what is it?"

"Sir, we have to go to the briefing. The signal alarm has been sounding for the last five minutes."

"Yes, of course."

He decided to make a call before he left the com room. "L1 to L3."

"Go ahead, EP I've been monitoring the situation. What can I do?"

Good old, Pump, he thought, always watching my back. "Thanks, Pump. Keep watch over the Urals and let me know when the cloud clears and when you receive a signal. Okay?"

"No worries, 'ol buddy. You'll be the first to know when I hear the first peep."

"I'll call you later."

"Roger that. L3 out."

Elvis took out the node and put it back in the sterile holder he'd taken it from and stood. He glanced down at the monitor. The boiling terrible clouds rolled steadily east across the Russian steppes toward it's opposite number coming from the west. It appeared the two clouds of destruction would meet over Japan and together burn those islands off the map.

Elvis sighed then headed for the door to the corridor and the lift. The meeting better not take long. He wanted to get back here as soon as possible.

*\*\**

Elvis arrived back in the communications center alone. The briefing had lasted two hours.

He slumped down into the empty chair and leaned forward and rested his elbows on the consol. He closed his eyes. He wanted to cry but he was dry and numb from the pain of loss.

Sixty people on L1 had committed suicide after they witnessed the devastation. No one believed they'd kill themselves when the psychologists told them there would be suicides after impact. But he wasn't one of them. He agreed with the captain.

There was still hope that some of them would survive to carry on the human race.

While it was still early the news wasn't all bad.

None of the bunkers had yet made contact. And L2 hadn't checked in yet. But in addition to their station, L3, 4 and 5 were safe and the smaller asteroids following the planet killer hadn't yet been detected anywhere near the LaGrange orbits.

Elvis made a mental note when he got through to the Urals he'd ask Ivan if he'd heard from Simone on L2. He needed to stay optimistic.

The gardens and farms on the stations and the water and air purification systems made the LaGrange stations completely self-sufficient. They could survive and in twenty or thirty years they might even be able to join the survivors on the Earth to begin rebuilding civilization. At least that was the plan.

He wondered now if it was worth it for him. The chances Yvette survived the destruction in the Urals was slim. Even though it was unlikely he'd ever see her in person again any glimmer of hope that she lived was all he had to hold onto right now.

Just as he placed the com node in his ear the screen to his left blurred then steadied. It was the feed from L3 still focused on the Urals. His heart seemed to skip a beat and he gasped when he saw the blink of bright red lights from beneath the clouds still obscuring the mountain range.

"L1 to L3. Come in, Pumper! Please come in!" He realized he was shouting but his excitement had bubbled over.

"Yeah, E I'm here. But don't scream at me, pal. What's up?"

"Did you see that?"

"What?"

Elvis edged forward in his chair and looked hard at the monitor. The light had disappeared there were only clouds now. "Uuh, I saw a light. A red flashing light."

"I don't see anything," said Pumper. "Let me run back the recording."

The cameras images were recorded in a protein based memory storage system containing 150 billion yottabytes of information. This memory capacity had been installed in each station so the collective knowledge of mankind would remain intact for ten million years.

"Yes, you're right. There it is. Interesting."

Elvis wanted to jump through the consol his impatience threatened to overwhelm him. "Well, what do you think?"

"Let me check. Give me a few seconds."

Silence. Elvis blinked away beads of sweat that trickled into his eyes and he fidgeted in his chair as if it had suddenly become uncomfortable. Since the chair automatically formed to the contours of the person sitting it this was impossible, but he could barely contain his nerves. Yvette could be alive somewhere down there and someone could be trying to signal them.

"Hummm, E, my holo interface tells me this is a signal. A signal of human origin."

"What does it say?" Elvis blurted.

'Well, it's in Morse code..." Pumper's voice trailed off.

"Never mind all that. Is it from my wife?"

"Huh, no, E. It's an automated signal the computer was programmed to look for if the bunker…" Again his voice trailed off.

"You mean the message was to be sent if the bunker survived?"

"Huh, no. The opposite I'm afraid." Pumper paused. "I'm so sorry, E," he said his voice a whisper.

Elvis' shoulders slumped and a wave of grief washed over him in waves. She was dead. It was over. "Thanks, Pump."

He signed off and asked Maple to signal his shift replacement to take over for him. She did as he asked without question.

"I'll be in my cabin," he said before leaving the communications center.

Elvis arrived back in his cabin and sat down heavily on the bunk. He wondered what he'd do now. How would he carry on without the knowledge his beloved Yvette was alive and well? He shook his head and waited for the tears that would never come. He'd shed enough tears today.

He looked up and saw the monitor on the desk flash that a message was waiting for him. He didn't want to talk to anyone right now. All he needed was to be alone with his thoughts and his memories.

It was all he had left.

He shrugged. There was no harm in checking the message. Whoever it was would have to wait for a reply but he could at least listen.

"Play message," he whispered.

The screen came to life and his eyes grew wide. It was Yvette.

"Hi, E. It's me. I left this message for you a month ago when I was told the chances of survival were less than five percent." She paused and her watery, sky-blue eyes drifted to her right away from the camera then abruptly directly into the screen. It was as if she were looking right into his heart.

Elvis swallowed the bile that had risen to the back of his throat and let a breath slowly escape from between his dry lips. His hands trembled and a knot formed in his stomach. She looked so beautiful, so vulnerable.

"I love you, E. I always have and if there is another world beyond this one then I will wait for you as long as it takes. But I want you to do something for me. I want you to stay alive and help others to stay alive."

She paused again and her lips trembled. "And I want you to donate sperm to help the human race survive.

"I'm asking you to do this because if you and other the men and women who survive don't do this then the human races very existence will have been for nothing. I don't believe that and I know you don't believe it either.

"Please, Elvis, please promise me you'll do this. Please. And always remember, I love you."

The screen went dark.

He started when there was a knock on his door. He wiped the back of his hand across his eyes stood and walked to the door. He tapped the keypad next to the door.

The cabin door slid aside to reveal Maple standing in the corridor. Her brown eyes were slightly sad. He knew it wasn't real emotion but he appreciated the effort anyway.

"Yes, Maple what is it?"

"We just received word that L2 was damaged in a meteor shower, but they have managed to effect repairs and made contact a few minutes ago. No reported injuries."

Elvis nodded. "That is good news. Thanks, M."

The hologram nodded. "Yes, sir. I thought you'd like to know right away."

Elvis smiled at Maple then tapped the keypad next to the door and it closed.

Elvis walked to the desk where the monitor rested and sat on the chair facing the monitor. He stared at the screen.

Yes, he decided he'd do what Yvette wanted. She was right. He had a responsibility to humankind far greater than himself.

And he'd do it for Yvette.

# T.I.N. MEN

THE U.S. ARMY ISSUED ergonomic chair beneath Technical Sergeant Will Arnett trembled. Uncertain what was happening, Will's eyes drifted to the half empty glass of coke he'd earlier placed on the cup holder recessed into the console next to his elbow.

Or was it half full? He'd always hated pop psychology, and was far too practical for such limited cerebral arguments. In his civilian life he had a PhD in software engineering. He programmed software. Everything in the world was either a one or a zero, nothing more.

He watched the sweet brown liquid splash up along the sides of the glass then his hazel eyes flitted sharply back to the three screens recessed into the console in front of him. The deck shuddered again, only more violently this time. The screens provided him a 360-degree view of the dry cactus and scrub brush dotting the Arizona landscape surrounding the Styker reconnaissance vehicle.

He swallowed hard and his eyes went wide as an unbelievable site appeared on the center screen. He would later say he'd seen as a silver and gray robot that the on-board sensors said was over sixty feet in height suddenly appear out of the gloom of first light. Its body was human shaped with a wide chest and a head that swiveled as it scanned the desert. It moved in giant footsteps each the length of a Cadillac. It was headed westerly ninety degrees from his position.

It was barely past sunrise and the blue velvet sky glowed orange, yellow, and red as the sun's tendrils chased away the night. Since the desert can play tricks on you at sunrise Will blinked a few times, but the robot didn't vanish. *Impossible. I must be dreaming. If it's real though it'd sure be fascinating.*

Will had been on watch all night in the Styker on a military exercise in this patch of barren desert. As day approached he'd begun to wonder who he'd pissed off to rate this duty. Fortunately the Styker was a nuclear, biological, chemical reconnaissance vehicle, or NBCRV. This meant if they were properly equipped (which they were not) the five-person crew could survive inside this tin can for up to two weeks.

Will's heart beat hard in his chest and he fought the urge to bolt from his chair as the massive robot on the screen took a step closer. The vehicle bounced on its undercarriage.

With trembling fingers, Will pulled down the mouth mike attached to his armored helmet he'd pushed out of his way. He needed to contact Lieutenant Sims in the command cab up front. The mike was voice activated, "Huh, sir."

No response.

"Sir! Lieutenant!"

The ground shook as the robot increased its pace. It occurred to Will the Stryker might not withstand being crushed underfoot by this mechanical monster. He didn't know why he thought this, but this robot's appearance had created an unusual situation after all.

"Yeah," came the sleepy reply of the Lieutenant who was sitting in the driver compartment forward of the surveillance control center. There was a hatch between the control center and the driver's compartment, which the LT kept locked when he was up front with the driver.

The colonel had sent them out with himself, the lieutenant, and a rookie private named Pike as driver, on what he called a training mission.

The mission objective was to simulate the loss of crew members to test how resourceful they could be with only three remaining crew versus a normal compliment.

Will swallowed hard when he recalled they didn't even have .50 cal ammunition for the M2 machine gun.

"What is it, grunt?" came the annoyed reply.

Will cringed. Sims was regular Army. He was reserves so Sims rode him pretty hard whenever the opportunity presented itself. "Sir, there's a giant robot coming straight at us. Sir." He added the second sir, because he knew how ludicrous what he'd just said sounded.

He watched the robot stop then the dark pupiless eyes set in the human shaped head swiveled and seemingly look right at him through the video screen. The remaining moisture in his mouth evaporated.

"A robot?" Sims grunted. "You bin watching cartoons back there?"

"Huh, no, sir. Believe me it's real. Turn on the external lights. Sir."

"OK, grunt, but if you've woken me for nothin' I'm gonna kick your ass all the way back ta base." Will heard the sound of a toggle switch through his headset.

"What the...." Sims voice trembled. "Pike! Wake up! Get us the hell outta here, we —"

Sims voice was cut off when every screen went dark and the familiar hum of the air exchange died. Will held his breath as he waited for the emergency generator to kick in, but nothing happened. They were dead in the water. Will sat in darkness. His breathing became shallow. The air already seemed stuffy and a few degrees warmer. A trickle of sweat ran down his left cheek and back beneath his undershirt.

This is impossible. The M1135 NBC Reconnaissance Vehicle, or Stryker, was designed to be impervious to Electro Magnetic Pulse attack. The exterior hull was constructed from titanium alloy. Sloped armor would deflect an EMP attack. The interior walls were lined with a rubber liner to absorb electricity. The hull was also shielded from radiation by sealed lead paint, and the vehicle had its own internal air and recycling filtration system so a gas attack would be useless.

They were as safe as anyone on earth from non-conventional attack could be. Unfortunately, since the armor plating on the sides was thin, only 14 millimeters thick, conventional weapons, or a giant robot foot, could easily destroy them.

Will said a silent prayer. He was about to die.

The vehicle around him trembled then he winced at the awful screech of metal on metal. He was gripped by a feeling of weightlessness. The vehicle around him shuddered as it was lifted into the air. His stomach muscles tighten as nausea enveloped him.

Will reached out to grip the edge of the consol and held on as tightly as he was able. Whatever was happening was causing his lean frame to alternate between straining against the restraining strap across his chest, he'd been insightful enough to have on, and weightless as if he were floating in a swimming pool.

Fear welled from his belly as he realized the robot must have picked up the Stryker and was carrying it as if it were a child's toy. But where were they going?

***

After half an hour the swaying stopped and the vehicle bounced once more as it was placed on the ground. Will who's heart still pounded rapidly in his chest, and he were frozen in his chair his sweaty fingers in a death grip on the chair arms. They'd stopped moving. Will let out a breath he'd been holding.

He didn't much care where on terra firma he was, just that the shaking had stopped. He let out a breath he'd been holding and wiped his brow with the sleeve of his uniform jumper.

So far the robot hadn't threatened them.

"You in the M1135," said a booming mechanical voice over his headset. "Come out or we will destroy you."

Okay, that sounded like a threat. But who was we?

In the last thirty minutes, Will had mapped out a plan of action in his head. The robot was tall; it's hands were probably twenty feet or more from the ground. If he got out and took off running he would run between its legs before it could react. He'd find a hiding place where the robot was too large to follow until he could find a radio or a telephone to call the base. What are my options?

The Stryker didn't have any surface-to-robot missiles, hand grenades, or as much as firecracker for that matter, so he couldn't fight the thing. Stryker vehicles only have the M2 for defensive purposes. And he couldn't surrender that would be cowardice in the face of the enemy. If he survived the idea of spending time in a Leavenworth prison cell made him the ultimate coward.

The army really hated the word surrender. His superiors would not be amused.

No. All he could do was run for his life. To fight another day of course. It was a strategic retreat.

Somehow he didn't think a giant robot that seized U.S. Army property was a friendly so it had to be fought. America was the land of shoot-first-ask-questions-later. That much was clear. But he didn't think of himself as the man for the job. I'm a software engineer, not a warrior.

The real questions were, how did a giant robot get into the middle of the Arizona desert, and why was it here?

He rose on unsteady legs from the chair and took in a deep breath to try and settle his nerves. His cheeks puffed out as he released his breath in stuttering gasps. He wiped the sweat from his brow with the back of his hand.

The emergency escape hatch was at the rear of the control center. He stumbled across the deck his hands reaching out in front of him. Quickly his fingertips made contact with the smooth walls of the vehicle. He managed to make his way to where he recalled the hatch was located without falling over one of the chairs at the workstations. He yelped as the toe of his right boot struck the hatch.

He winced and swallowed hard.

Geez, that hurts.

The pain gradually subsided until finally he knelt down and felt for the hatch release. He found it and pulled the handle toward him. The hatch swung in and the control center was suddenly awash in blinding light. He closed his eyes tightly and waited for his vision to clear.

Holding one hand up to shield his eyes he blinked but managed to squeeze out the hatch without falling. *At least I can keep some of my dignity.*

So far his escape plan hadn't worked so well. He couldn't run blindly unable to see where he was headed could he?

"Stay right where you are, Sergeant." The voice was deep but mechanical.

Knowing a threat when he heard one Will froze and waited. He suspected if it meant to kill him he would already be dead.

His eyesight gradually began to clear, enough so he could make out fuzzy shapes. One he expected the other he did not.

The forbidding very tall, very wide shape had to be the robot. Beside the large blob of fuzz was a smaller more human sized shape. And it had curves. Female curves.

What the...? Where am I?

"You ok, Sergeant?" said the woman.

Will blinked and the woman came into sharper focus. She was dressed in blue jeans, sneakers, and wore a bright orange tee shirt with the words Mr. Fuzz emblazoned across her full breasts.

"Name's Arnett. Will Arnett. Technical Sergeant, United States Army. Serial number —"

She laughed cutting him off in his name-rank-and-serial-number spiel. He had never been given an order to only provide these details, but he'd seen enough movies to know this was the procedure when captured by the enemy.

At least they seemed to be an enemy. He eyed the shapely woman with her laughing blue eyes, dimple in her right cheek, and smirk on her lips. Funny thing was she wasn't acting like an enemy.

"Huh, sorry," he said. "That was about as stupid as I feel right now." She chuckled. He detected the scent of lemons coming from her direction. "I think it was kind of cute actually."

"I have a question for you," Will said.

She smiled and held up a tablet reader she'd been holding in her left hand.

"Everything you need to know is on here. If you follow me we'll get some breakfast while you read."

Will frowned. She was avoiding the obvious and he was getting pissed off. "OK, I'll agree but you have to tell me your name first."

She shook her head. "I'm sorry. We don't get many visitors so my social skills are somewhat lacking. My name's Holly Hope. I'm a scientist, like you."

\*\*\*

The walked down the well-lit corridor toward what appeared to be elevator doors at more than twenty feet away. *Where am I?* he wondered.

"Are we underground?" he asked.

Holly nodded. "Oh, yes, about a mile down actually."

Will let go with a soft whistle. *Good thing I'm not claustrophobic.*

What was lighting the corridor wasn't obvious, but he suspected the ceiling was painted with a florescent paint back-lit by low wattage light tubes. This told him they were trying to conserve power. Interesting.

He wondered if they could generate enough power to fuel a sixty-foot tall robot why they needed to conserve power. He mentally filed the information away.

"So, Holly, where are my lieutenant, and the driver?" So far, Holly had been relaxed and wore an easy smile on her lips. She wasn't armed as far as he could tell, but she had made him curious, especially when she revealed she had a PhD in biotechnology. And somehow she knew he was had a PhD in software engineering.

He frowned. How does she know so much about me? He looked at her walking beside him. She was sure cute, and apparently smart. He liked those qualities in a woman.

"Randall will drop them back on the spot in the desert where he picked you up," she said as casually as if she'd just made a run to the corner store for a candy bar. "No need to worry about them. They'll be fine."

He looked at her. "Who's Randall?"

She chuckled. Is everything I say funny? I know I'm not funny.

"Sorry. The robot that brought you here. His name's Randall." She used one index finger to make a twirling motion next to her head. "I can be so spiny sometimes.

I forget you haven't been here before. Randall is one of our 'bots."

Will swallowed and his stomach tightened. "One?"

"Yeah. I mean, yes." They had reached the elevator doors. Affixed to the wall next to the doors was a black proximity reader. It had ridges in its surface but was otherwise devoid of any markings.

Holly pulled a white plastic card about the size of a credit card from her right pocket and swiped it over the prox card reader. The elevators doors parted. She stuffed the card back in her pocket then her eyes locked on his.

"You ready?"

Will swallowed hard. "For what?"

The sides of her mouth curled slightly but her eyes became flat. The humor had left her as if the air in a balloon had been slowly released. It unnerved him.

"To see the most incredible things you have ever seen."

Will wondered what she meant, but the scientist in him boiled to the surface. He had to know where that robot came from and where he was and who was behind this. Holly didn't have the specialty to build the robot that carried him here. Wherever here was.

Once she told him about her specialty, being chemical engineering, he knew there had to have been others involved.

A knot of excitement shredded the fear he'd felt earlier. Like Mulder and Scully he had to know the truth.

"Yes, Holly, I am ready."

Her features changed back to the friendly grin and her eyes sparkled as they had before. "Great. You must meet, Dr. Good."

Will nodded.

They entered the elevator and the doors closed behind them. Holly used the card to swipe over another proximity card reader. There were no buttons and no floor numbers. The walls were bare except for the card reader.

There was a slight sensation of movement that was barely detectable. Will wondered if they were moving at all.

Holly became his tour guide. "We'll be traveling to the underground living quarters and research facilities twenty stories underground. The quarters house up to twenty-seven research scientists.

"We have specialists who are experts in their fields; chemistry, biology, propulsion, exobiology, bioelectronics, biomechanics, and engineers in the fields of aerospace, and chemical engineering. We also have several PhD's who worked at JPL on interplanetary exploration."

"Is there a brochure?" Will muttered.

Holly looked at him with one eyebrow raised and laughed. "I like you already. You're funny."

The elevator stopped. The doors slid open. Will's jaw dropped. The vast expanse reminded him of his favorite '50's science fiction movie, Forbidden Planet.

The area was vast with diamond shaped corridors leading off a central common area teaming with people, some riding four-wheeled electric trucks and others wearing white lab coats carrying tablets and what looked like cell phones, though he suspected the devices weren't cell phones. This far underground the most powerful cell on the commercial market wouldn't be able to receive a signal.

The floors were polished black rock with veins of color running through it. And there were quite a number of robots. Not as big as the one that had snatched him, they were at least six feet tall and shiny silver in color.

They had no eyes but must have sensors because they moved easily amongst the humans, who took no interest in them. It was as if robots were normal.

*I'm clearly not in Kansas anymore.* Or Arizona to be exact.

"I told you," Holly said as she exited the elevator ahead of him.

Will regained his composure and chased after her as she led him across the vast central hub. She was right. This was incredible. He caught up with her as she continued her tour guide spiel. She explained that the corridors led to the laboratories, the recreation area, a cafeteria and the living quarters. "We're going to the directors office first. Dr. Good is anxious to meet you."

Will noticed above each corridor was a large illuminated capital letter. They were about to enter corridor D. "Who is this, Dr. Good?"

"He's the director of the project. He has four PhD's, and has been director of the project since it started in 1967."

"Oh, really?" Will refrained from rolling his eyes. Good was an old man, probably with old man ideas. A robot walked past them in the corridor. Well, maybe not that old.

They passed several men and women who nodded to Holly as they went by but seemed to ignore him. They seemed a cold, unfriendly bunch.

He wondered now why he was here.

Finally they arrived outside a door recessed into the side of the corridor. There was no door handle or lock. Beside it was another prox card reader.

Holly glanced at him and offered a closed mouth smile. She swiped her card over the reader and the door slid open and receding into the door frame.

Beyond the entrance was a well-lit office with a glass desk (he recognized it was made of plexi-glass not real glass. His old prof used to have one just like it). The desk had a flat screen in one corner and a pen set in a wooden holder near the front edge of the desk. The two items could not be more dissimilar. The old clashed with the new.

Two red leather chairs sat in front of the desk. Against one wall to his right was a matching red leather sofa. Hung on the wall over the sofa was a painting of the Saturn V rocket in flight.

They entered the office together with Holly slightly ahead as the lead.

Sitting behind the desk sipping a dark liquid from glass was a small man. He looked about the size of a ten year old, only the steel gray hair that ringed his bald spot, and the wrinkles around the intense green eyes told Will he was much older than he at first appeared.

"Sit down, Sergeant," the man said, his tone gentle but firm. Will sat down burying his hands in his lap to hide the trembling. "I'm sorry about the dramatic manner of your arrival, but it couldn't be helped."

Maybe this was a bad idea after all.

"I'm Dr. Oz Good. You can call me, Dr. Good." He set the glass on the desk. His eyes narrowed and his smooth brow creased by a frown. "Never call me the Wizard of Oz."

Holly struggled in vain to stifle a snort. When she did let go, Dr. Good's eyes shot to her and he scowled. "Leave us, Dr. Hope." His tone was tight and disapproving.

Will looked at Holly. Her cheeks were flushed red and her eyes avoided the director's glare. She nodded her head slightly then said, "Yes, sir. I've got to check my most recent test results anyway." Holly turned left the office the door sliding closed behind her.

Dr. Good's features relaxed and he steepled his fingers and seemed to be studying him. Will was startled and jumped in the chair when Dr. Good suddenly burst out laughing. He squirmed until Dr. Good stopped and wiped the tears from his eyes with his long thin fingers. "So, Sergeant. I'm told you have a PhD in software engineering?"

Will cleared his throat. He prayed he wouldn't sound like a frog. "Uhhh, yes sir, Dr. Good...sir." I sound like the biggest idiot on the planet.

"Good. Great in fact. We need a person with your qualifications."

He paused and the smile dissipated as his expression shifted to somber. "The last software engineer was...lost." He stood up behind the desk. Will detected the hesitation in Dr. Good's voice.

Something bad must have happened, but what? "So you want me to work for you?"

Good smiled, walked around the desk, and moved to sit on the sofa. He waved to Will to join him. Will sat down. "Yes, but it's up to you. Of course I will have to explain what this is all about, and about our mission."

Will nodded. "Of course." This sounds a bit cryptic. He needed answers. "Where are we?" he asked.

"I assume you've heard of Area 51?" Will nodded again and licked his lips. Aliens. These guys are nuts. "We are Area 52. Our facility, our mission, our funding, our existence is above top secret. The only people who know about us are at the top of the U.S. government. The President, the Secretary of Defense, and the Chairman of the Joint Chiefs."

His eyes narrowed and his lips formed a thin line. "No one else." He rose to his feet and began to pace the tiled floor. "Other than those who work here of course.

No one knows about us, or must know about us."

Will's heart beat faster at that last part. If he told anyone about this place and the robots, he had a feeling it wouldn't be good for his health. "Ummm, Dr. Hope said something about a project?"

Dr. Good stopped pacing and turned to face him. "Our project is called TIN Men."

"By the name I'm guessing you build robots?"

Good arched one eyebrow. "That's only half the story actually."

Will arched an eyebrow. "What's the other half?"

"We're in a robot race that's been going on since 1967."

Will's curiosity threatened to bubble over. "Robot race? Like a marathon?"

Dr. Good laughed and crossed his arms over his narrow chest. "No. Not that kind of race. A cold war style race." Good dropped into silence.

Will stared back at Dr. Good uncertain what or whom he was talking about. Russia wasn't the USSR, in fact the country was a shell of it's former self.

China was an economic power. Sure, they had a large military, but funding an ultra secret robot program seemed a little beyond their means. Iraq? Iran? No. No way. The Saudi's, the North Koreans? The European Union? Unlikely. "A cold war? With whom?"

"Who do you think?"

Will shrugged. "I don't know...Japan?"

Dr. Good's eyebrows rose in obvious surprise. "How did you know that?"

"I guessed."

Dr. Good moved across to this desk and picked up his glass of coke. He took a swig and offered Will a glass, which he accepted. After he filled a glass from the bottle in the bar fridge behind his desk he sat once again in the red leather executive chair.

He explained. "As you know Japan has become a technologically advanced society. Many Japanese have a love for science fiction, and robots, and giant monsters. They started a giant robot program, so in order for the United States to keep it's technological edge we began ours at the same time."

Will snorted. "You do realize how stupid that sounds, right?"

"Yes, I know. But we have been in a race with the Japanese ever since. There are unconfirmed rumors that India and China have begun early work on their own robot programs, but our latest intelligence reports say they're years away from a practical working prototype."

Will stood he'd had enough. "You know this all sounds crazy. We're talking about robots!" He moved to the desk and stood staring at Dr. Good. "It's science fiction. It's not real."

Dr. Good eased back in his chair causing the leather to squeak. He arched an eyebrow. "You met, Randall, and saw the worker drones in the corridors did you not?"

Will grimaced. He was right of course. As unbelievable as it sounded the robots were real. But was everything else he said also true? "OK, Dr. Good, I'll concede that point, but I find it hard to believe a robot cold war has been going on for over forty years, and no one knows about it."

"We have developed a drug that wipes selected memories of anyone who comes into contact with our facility or research."

Will sensed Good was hiding something from him, though hiding wasn't the correct term. A better term would be evasion.

He wasn't answering his questions directly. For the first time in a long time, Will knew he was being tested. And this made him mad. He'd hated tests since Mrs. Chopnik sprang that surprise arithmetic test on his first grade class.

"Listen, Dr. Good, let's stop beating around the mechanical bush and you tell me what's going on and why I'm here."

Dr. Good surprised him when his narrow features broke into a wide smile. Had he said something funny? Or had he just sounded so stupid all a person could do was laugh at him.

"Dr. Arnett, welcome aboard." He stood behind his desk and held out his right hand.

Will took Dr. Good's hand in his. His skin was warm and the grip was firm. But what had he just joined? Will released his grip and sat down again. "Dr. Good, please tell me something important. I've come aboard what exactly?" He blurted out the last word. His frustration meter had gone through the roof.

Dr. Good's expression became very serious. "I'm offering you a chance to join Project TIN Men as the lead software development engineer. It is quite an honor, believe me.

You'll lead a team of ten of the best software engineers in the world, and you'll be paid more than Google or Microsoft or Facebook would ever pay you. I can say with no exaggeration in one year you'll make enough to buy your own private island. And you'll have enough money to buy a lifetime supply of those chocolate mint patties you love so much. Honestly? You could buy the company that makes those confections."

Will took a sip of the coke and then dragged in a deep breath. The soda tickled his taste buds and its sweetness lingered in tongue even after he swallowed. He released the breath, "What's the catch?"

Dr. Good's lips formed a tight smile. "Good. Direct. I like that." He paused and looked away. With his back now to Will he said, "We will transplant your brain into the body of a robot much like Randall so you won't require air or water. Not where you're going. Then you'll travel to the moon where you'll help to build a base on the dark side of the moon."

Will's heart raced. Moon base? His brain?

\*\*\*

Two months later, Will lay on an operating table waiting for the electrodes to be affixed to the four input terminals surgically implanted in his skull. The terminals were inserted into his frontal lobe, parietal lobe, occipital lobe, and temporal lobe. His brain wouldn't actually be removed and placed in the robots control center, but somehow the scientific team had found a way to transfer every experience, every memory, and every instruction accumulated in his lifetime to the robots artificial brain.

His body would be stored in stasis while he went to the moon. The dark side of the moon to be exact. The team would be composed of seventeen robots and the base would take six months to complete.

He was pleased, Holly would be accompanying him, her transferred brain also encased in a robot body.

He'd been fully briefed on the mission. They were to build a base on the dark side of the moon hidden from Earthly eyes. The reason he'd been given was the base was being built by an international organization funded by the G25. The funding was secret and the project was secret. The organization was code named The International Network or T.I.N.. The code name for the bot's was TIN Men.

He was not only chosen for his expertise in his field, but because his parents died in a car accident two years ago, he was an only child, and had no other family.

He'd begun to enjoy being a part of something. In the army he had felt more like an outsider, the regular grunts detested soldiers who were smarter than they were.

To be honest most gerbils were smarter than most of the men and women he served with in the recon unit he'd been assigned to.

While for the most part the story rang true, Will, still thought there were gaps in the tale that bothered him. Holly had admitted her reservations as well after they'd slept together. She had been working at MIT when she was approached and asked to join the project. She'd agreed when she was advised Dr. Good was the project director.

An interesting factoid about her was she was also an orphan like himself. In fact everyone he'd encounter involved with the project had no family. He couldn't shake the uncomfortable thought this meant they wouldn't be missed if something went wrong.

But what could go wrong? Their brains were transferred to living machines, and then they'd slip through an energy field that transmitted matter thousands of miles in the blink of an eye.

A matter transmitter terminal was already on the moon near the site where the base would be constructed.

The European-China Space Agency had sent a robot spacecraft with the terminal aboard to the moon and by all reports it landed safely. Some worker droids were to set up the terminal. Recent orbital surveys confirmed the droids had completed the set up. But the real question was had the droids put it together properly.

The worker droids could have built the moon base as well, but it would have taken them decades due to their limited ability to adjust to unexpected situations. They were only capable of being programmed to respond to pre-determined situations. And not every situation could be covered by the programmers

Dr Good had been evasive about why they needed to work so fast and take such risks, but Will suspected there was much more going on.

Also, any breakdowns wouldn't be fixed; the resources hadn't been supplied to fix any mechanical problems if the droids broke down. Yet.

But this was all about to change. The plan was for the TIN men to build a repair facility as the first phase of the project.

"All TIN men to the departure bay!" said a deep male voice over the facility wide public address system.

Will set the giant robot in motion and walked the massive tunnels headed for the departure bay. Holly's lime green and soft gray two-tone bot joined him. He was pleased to see her.

"Hi, Holly, you ready?"

Her bot swiveled its head to face his and nodded. "For sure. But I wish they'd refer to us females as TIN women."

We'd been having this discussion for months but it was a spurious argument because the robots were sexless. The human sexual urges and feelings of the brain implanted in the artificial brain weren't relevant. Especially as we communicated by telepathic means and were about to enter an inhospitable environment. In such a place sex where wasn't relevant, and these bodies weren't built with the right bits and pieces anyway.

"Next time, Ok?" Will joked.

Holly chuckled. "Yeah, okay."

We soon arrived in the departure bay where the transport technician had set up the first test of the matter transmitter. There were going to be five tests before they were sent through.

First they would send a Camera and Recording Bot, or CRB, to monitor the reception terminal.

The CRB central processor and sealed camera was built on a platform set on rubber composite tracks. Immediately upon arrival on the moon it would move off the platform then send pictures back of the remaining tests. Of course if no signals came back this would mean the droids had failed to set up the receiving transport receiver properly.

Will watched the technicians guide the robot onto the large round platform that rose above the shiny tile floor of the bay. Near the outer walls were five consoles where technicians sat monitoring everything from energy levels of the matter transporters systems, to humidity, and the telemetry data provided by a satellite net transmitted from high Earth orbit to a network of satellites orbiting the moon. This would be their lifeline until the job was complete for Will and Holly and the rest of the team. There were going to be six of us building the station.

Will and Holly watched as the technicians called out data they received from their consoles as a humming sound began to grow in intensity. Finally the humming reached its zenith and there was a brilliant flash of light that seemed to consume the CRB. When the light dissipated the bot was gone.

"Sir!" It was one of the telemetry technicians calling to Dr. Good who stood across the room at another console watching the power level indicators. He was really proud of the fact they had finally harnessed the power of a nuclear reactor that generated more power than the Hiroshima bomb. He'd been working on it since the project began in 1967.

Dr. Good looked up. "Yes? What is it, Jamal?"

"Sir. There is no signal from the CRB."

Dr. Good's brow wrinkled and Will recognized the confusion on his narrow features. "Give it a few minutes."

Suddenly the technician yelled out. His face paled and he waved one hand wildly at the screen in his console. "Sir. You better come look at this."

Dr. Good nodded and stuffed his hands in the pockets of his ankle length white lab coat. He walked casually across the room seemingly unconcerned about the urgency in Jamal's tone. Will noted his brow was knitted and he was humming, both signs he was in reality worried. Will sensed something bad had happened.

Will moved his robot body closer to the console and at an angle he could see the screen. What he saw made him for the first time reconsider his reasons for agreeing to be part of this project.

On the screen he could see a wide view of a field of gray rock and sand under an ink black sky dotted with points of unblinking light. There were also blackened shards of metal scattered like leaves across the moon's surface. From the angle of the image Will suspected the camera was on its side.

It was clearly evidence of an explosion. Now Will was worried.

The only thing that could explode was the nuclear power source for the transmitter reception terminal, and the internal power source for the droids. The good thing was the camera aboard the CBR had survived the explosion, which meant the mostly likely source of the explosion was a droid.

The root of this problem was how this had happened. Was it coincidental the arrival of the CBR occurred at the exact moment of a droid exploding? And did the explosion damage the transporter terminal?

Dr. Good crossed his arms and studied the screen his features scrunched in a scowl. "I wasn't expecting this so soon."

"Dr. Good," piped up Holly's bot. She had approached the console from the opposite side from where Will was standing. "What were you expecting?"

Will thought her tone was harsh, but he too was surprised Dr. Good had withheld information from them. "Yes, doc, Holly and I want what's going on."

Dr. Good sighed and his shoulders sagged. He took off his wire-rimmed glasses and massaged the bridge of his nose with his thumb and forefinger as if he had a headache. His eyes were closed. Suddenly he stopped and grunted as he put his glasses back on.

He reached for the com system button on the console and punched the red button, which changed to green meaning the public address system had been activated.

"Attention all TIN Men Project personnel, this is Dr. Good." He paused and took in a deep breath then continued. "I've been asked a rather important question and while I'm forbidden to reveal certain facts recent events on the moon lead me to believe you must all know why we must build the base on the moon and maintain absolute secrecy.

"I'm certain you have all been wondering about the rumored hidden agenda. I appreciate you have all followed orders without question while bringing this project to fruition. If we fail in our endeavors we, meaning all of humanity, will be faced with a future too terrible to imagine at the hands of a megalomaniac bent on total world domination.

Dr. Good glanced at Will's bot then his eyes drifted to Holly's. "Our TIN Men will be the front line in this war.

A war against a secret organization calling itself The Mayday Directorate. The leader of The Mayday Directorate is a brilliant scientist named Dr. Bartholomew Good, my brother."

\*\*\*

Will heaved the large gray and black rock across the moonscape. In the one sixth Earth gravity it flew more than a thousand yards before landing in a cloud of moon dust. They had nearly finished clearing the area where they'd sink the foundation posts for the new base within a couple of hours. Will and the rest of the TIN Men had only been here for ten hours and already the base construction was well underway.

Holly was with a team of the surviving droids extracting ice from the shaded sides of craters. They would place the ice in the evaporation tank two of their colleagues were busily constructing. Once the tank was powered up the ice would melt and provide fresh water for the base's eventual inhabitants.

They'd waited for three months until a force of armed TIN Men could be built to provide security for the base construction. Will wasn't happy to see an armed presence but The Mayday Directorate had been prevented from doing any further sabotage.

It was discovered that their agents had planted bombs inside some of the worker droids. Though a couple exploded when the CBR went through the matter transporter they hadn't damaged the device so severely as to stop the transport of a repair crew for the droids.

After the repairs Will, Holly and the rest of the team had been sent to the moon and work had begun.

Dr. Good explained that his brother and he had started the project at Area 52 together, but his brother and he had a falling out. He hadn't heard of his brother until The Directorate destroyed the Columbia space shuttle.

Once the moon base was completed it would begin its real work. It would be the jumping off point to send deep space missions throughout the solar system to find minerals and water and other building blocks for the eventual exploration of planets where the first signs of extraterrestrial life had been discovered.

Will was excited about the future and hoped his TIN man would survive for many years to come so he could be part of the next great adventure. Humankind was going to finally make its mark in the galaxy.

Will stopped working when the ground began to shake.

He hoped it was a meteor strike but then the early warning meteor detection grid would have alerted them of an impending strike. He had a sinking feeling he knew what caused the disturbance of the moon's crust.

Suddenly the horizon lit up with gold and red flashes.

There was no denying it they were being attacked. And the TMD bots had used cloaking technology in the past but every time it had been scouts and they were quickly destroyed by the TIN Men security team. Somehow this felt different.

Will had to brace the bot's legs to keep from falling over when the ground heaved beneath him and a cloud of dust shot into the star studded sky to the west of his position. The gray dust quickly blocked out the stars. Will knew the weapon ports Dr. Good had installed in his robot were about to become useful. He had hoped to avoid the coming conflict. The Directorate didn't want to talk, they wanted to destroy. Now it was war.

The TMD was planning to stop them before they could complete the moon base. Holly told him they were paid by a coalition of pirate states led by the Texas Syndicate and the Welsh Dominion. They were paying TMD to destroy the TIN Men project.

They planned to take over the interstellar exploration of deep space, not for peaceful purposes, but for conquest and monopolizing resources.

They had to be stopped, and the TIN Men had to do it.

"Sentry Seven reporting a breach in the defensive line. There are three —"

The com went silent. Sentry Seven had been taken out."

It was time for action. Will sent a message through the com net. "Dr. Arnett to TIN Men and all sentries. Initiate plan alpha-two-nine."

Will counted the acknowledgments and realized fourteen sentries had been lost already. Will walked to the edge of worksite and stopped. Clouds of moon dust had risen to blot out the star field across the horizon.

He deployed the laser gun in the left arm of the robot then the rail gun with the armor piercing projectiles in the right arm. He also engaged the energy shield that he hoped would hold off the TMD bot's weapons long enough so he could launch a counter attack. Unfortunately the weapons had been deployed so quickly the testing of the shields had been inconclusive. Will shuddered at the memory of the chest plate of the test bot melting and fusing its torso.

The plan was to deploy the TIN Men and the surviving sentries in an oval shape to guard the base by repelling any attacks. The sentries were smaller therefore they'd be in front of the TIN Men who were taller and better armed. It was a classic order of battle design used by the British (though they used squares not ovals), and the Roman legions before them.

Soon Will counted thirty five sentries and looking around he saw his six companion TIN Men, including Holly who was directly behind him facing outward, her back to him. He worried she would get hit, but Dr. Good's armor should protect her. He hoped.

Then sentries quickly deployed per the plan and there was an uneasy lull. Silence no com traffic as they waited for the enemy. If Will's TIN Man could smell it would smell the sweat, the oil and grease and the heat of the laser warming to firing temperature. But since the suits didn't allow for such sensory data he could only imagine it these things.

Suddenly from over the horizon six large TMD robots appeared. Their armored bodies were black and silver and from the look of them they appeared to have missile launchers affixed to their left shoulders and rail guns attached to their right arms. This wasn't going to be an easy fight. Dr. Good had obviously anticipated the TIN Men's weapons and tactics.

This was further supported by their spreading out so as not to create one massive target. They'd be in range in ten seconds.

Time seemed to pass slower as Will silently counted down the seconds. His targeting scanner beeped and he pressed the firing button for the rail gun.

The first hardened steel/titanium projectile shot off the rail and tracked to the target, one of the enemy bots to his right. The projectile struck enemy bot in the center of its chest plate and it shot backward off its feet. It landed in a cloud of moon dust broken in half at the waist. The legs wouldn't work without the torso.

Will was pleased. One shot, one bot out of action. This wasn't going to be such a difficult battle after all.

A flash of a laser beam shot across the no mans land from one of the enemy bots. It struck Dr. Helen Taskers TIN Man and sliced her torso in two. It was almost as if her shields weren't on.

"Will." It was Holly. "I've picked up a low frequency wave that's interfering with our shield generators." She paused and the information sunk in. If the enemy was able to do this then maybe all of their systems could be compromised.

"Helen!" Will called.

"Yes," Helen said her voice trembling with fear.

"Check your generator power level."

There was a short pause then she replied, "It's reading zero. And it's not related to the damage I've sustained."

Now Will was worried.

The enemy had the upper hand, but the question was how had they learned to defeat their shields so easily? They still had the EMP weapon if the battle became hopeless. The electro magnetic pulse would take out the enemy, but would also immobilize the TIN Men. And it might wipe the neural connectors. Theoretically the EMP might result in brain death for the TIN Men as well as the enemy so it had to be a weapon of last resort. His orders from Dr. Good were simple: do not lose. He was in charge. He was determined to win this battle at all costs. The future was at stake.

A soft beep told him the enemy robots were now in range. He issued an order. "All TIN Men fire at will."

Will and the other TIN Men launched everything they had at the approaching enemy force. Their missiles and lasers struck the enemy bots and knocked them backward. The five remaining enemy robots were down. It had been easy — too easy."

"Cease fire," Will ordered.

When the first enemy robot suddenly stood up, Will's arterial heart rate increased. It looked unharmed from the missile impact.

Oh, oh, no champagne and caviar for us tonight. Celebrations for an easy victory would have to wait. They could shoot them again, but Will suspected this would be as ineffective as the first time.

"All TIN Men, stand your ground and be ready to deploy close quarter weapons." The acknowledgments came back as Will swapped out his laser for a ten-foot long titanium sword shaped blade. The others too had their bladed weapons at the ready.

The enemy robots had started moving again only this time they were covering more ground. They were taking long sustained strides. Will knew the other TIN Men would keep fighting until the end.

Another laser sliced Allisters robot in half at the waist. Will's mood darkened. He suspected now they had a plan. They were immobilizing the TIN Men but not destroying the fused human AI brain. They would transplant the fused brain into a new robot body they could control. It was the worst possible scenario. The loss of free will.

"Allister?"

"I'll be okay, Will. A little crazy glue and I'll be right as rain."

Will smiled inside. Allister was such a joker. "No, worries, old buddy. We'll get you fixed up as soon as we have these bastards taken care of."

"Thanks, Will."

Suddenly the enemy attacked.

Will fought back clashing with the nearest enemy bot. He quickly separated an arm from the upper torso of an enemy bot with a single swipe of his blade. It was then he noticed one of the enemy bots hanging back from the others. He watched with horror as it pressed a button on a panel on its right arm and suddenly he lost control of his body. Now he was a brain trapped in a non-functioning robot body. He was unable to move. *I have to move. I can't let them win.*

He stole a glance at Holly and saw she had retracted her blade and moved her robot to stand beside the enemy bot that had taken them all out of action. Will sent a command to the EMP weapon he'd secreted in one of the sentry bots. *No, not Holly!* Will wanted to cry.

His body jerked as if struck by lightning and the world around him disappeared.

*** 

When Will's systems came back on line he found himself lying on his back on the moon's surface staring up at the star strewn Milky Way galaxy. He tested his robot's limbs and found everything worked.

Getting to his feet he looked around and saw the remaining TIN Men were also getting to their feet. All expect, Holly who lay still on her back next to the leader of the TMD attack force.

He knew without asking their systems were fried and their AI brains along with all their memories were wiped clean.

Dr. Good had been correct. There was a traitor in their ranks, who had sabotaged the worker bots in an attempt to destroy the CBR thus jeopardizing the mission. And this same traitor provided the frequency of their shields to the enemy. Dr. Good hadn't thought they'd be able to do this unless they had help from an insider with the highest security level. Will didn't think anyone on the team could be a traitor. Especially not Holly. He'd been wrong.

Holly. Will didn't know why she did it, but one day he'd find out. When Holly's brain died her body stored in stasis back on Earth became an empty shell. She was gone forever.

Will was determined to ensure one day the other Dr. Good would pay for her death and the destruction he'd caused.

His Dr. Good and he knew they're robot bodies had been hardened against an EMP attack. The trap had worked perfectly.

It had brought the traitor out into the open. Too bad it turned out to be Holly.

"Will?" It was Allister.

"Don't worry, Allister, and you too, Helen. We'll get you both fixed up. I can't have you slacking off. We have a lot of work to do still."

Helen spoke next. "Sorry, about Holly, Will."

"It's no ones fault but hers," Will said and he meant it.

The TIN Men would survive and they would compete their task. Former Technical Sergeant Will Arnett was determined to make it happen.

# The Secret

HE HADN'T SLEPT MUCH in the past few days and he dreaded what the doctor would say when he saw him. A com whistle sounded interrupting his thoughts.

"Yes, sir?" Com officer Bell's gentle voice was at its best professional tone today. Allen smiled to himself. Alicia Bell was the best in the fleet, but he wasn't going to tell her that.

"Get me Admiral Smyth," said Allen. Smyth was in charge of ship assignments at Fleet HQ.

"Yes, sir I...."

Allen interrupted his communications officer. "Belay that Lieutenant...and Bell?"

"Yes, sir?"

"Thank you." Allen hit the com button again cutting off any further comment by his loyal communications officer.

Allen often relished the fact that his crew was so often behind him in difficult situations.

This time however they were asking too much of him, and in some ways he agreed with them. This time it was personal so he wanted to leave his crew out of it. Though he knew they wouldn't let this decision rest without a fight.

A hail from the control panel next to the door to his quarters interrupted his commiserations.

"Open," he said, his voice hollow in his ears. He knew who it was and he didn't need, or crave, advice.

The doors slid open with a whoosh and Dr. Sanji Kupta, his medical officer, waltzed in holding a bottle of what could only be brandy in his left hand. His haggard features were grim and the usual glint in his brilliant brown eyes was absent.

"Hanson," said Kupta, with a slight nod of his head as he sat in one of the empty chairs next to the desk.

Allen eyed Doc Kupta who sat in silence, the amber bottle with its curved neck sitting unopened next to him on the desks cool, dull gray surface. For his part Kupta seemed to be studying Allen as if he were one of his lab specimens.

"You know, Doc, I've never felt this way when a crew member is transferred. I mean for God's sake this isn't normal for a man in my position. They're demanding far too much of me this time."

Kupta crossed his thin arms across his narrow chest while a single dark, gray-streaked, eyebrow frowned at his captain.

"That's what worries me, Hanson."

Allen rose from his chair and began to pace the length of the cabin his booted footsteps dulled by the thick pile of the blue and gray carpet. His arms waved about as he spoke as if to accentuate his words.

Kupta watched in silence as his friend vented his anger and frustration.

Command had picked a fine time to eliminate the Captain's Yeoman program from the fleet's crew manifests.

Kelly Amstead, his yeoman of more than a year, was a close friend to many of the crew on-board, especially Bell, and extremely popular with everyone.

Consequently, the crew fully expected Allen, as captain of the *Earth's Daughter*, one of only fifteen such vessels in the fleet, to easily persuade command to have Amstead reassigned here, where she belonged.

After all Captain Hanson Allen had battled alien's aggressors, and survived strange spatial phenomena of all descriptions with distinction and valor and triumphed every time.

Surely a few stuffed shirts at command would be easily swept aside by their young, headstrong captain.

The rumor mill predicted Kelly would be back aboard within the week.

Deep down the doc suspected Allen had a more singular than altruistic reasons in mind than a simple question of leadership.

Naturally, Hanson Allen being Hanson Allen he'd made every effort to shield his personal feelings from all those around him. Kupta knew Hanson's true feelings for Kelly Amstead were buried somewhere deep inside him.

Hanson had always prided himself in his ability to keep his personal feelings concerning any one member of the crew from affecting his decisions. Fleet captains were expected to put the safety of the ship and its crew ahead of personal considerations. Kupta knew Hanson believed in this principal, but he also knew the man hated it.

There had been many times even he and First Officer Miller, as Hanson's best friends, were on the outside when it came to the captain's personal entanglements, and there had been many.

"Amstead has done so much to keep morale amongst this crew the highest in the fleet. Her work with those women on Synar II, and on other countless occasions is a credit to the service. She's the epitome of what the Star Force stands for.

Now they want her back at command? As what? Some admiral's desk jockey? Mark my words, Doc, I'm going to get to the bottom of this even if it means my command."

Doc snorted and shook his head. "You know you don't mean that, Hanson." He reached over and uncorked the bottle of brandy then reached into the hidden drawer where Hanson kept his glasses.

After retrieving two of the short clear glasses he poured two generous measures of the potent drink. The odor of sweet brandy filled the room. "Com'on have a drink with your doctor."

Hanson cast a disapproving glance at his long time friend then shrugged his broad shoulders and moved to the desk. He pulled out a second chair and sat down to face Kupta, a look of annoyance in his blue eyes.

"I don't need any lectures, Doc."

Kupta gave Allen a lopsided grin as he held up both hands in surrender. "No argument here. This is social call. After all I'm a doctor not a bartender. You need advice you go back to that little bar on Argelius III."

Allen let slip a small smile at Kupta's mention of the pleasure planet they'd visited years before. His expression softened.

He picked up the glass of brandy and downed the contents in one swallow. His face registered the heat of the alcohol as the burning liquid slid down his throat. "Of course you're right, doctor." He sighed heavily then with the thumb and index finger of his right hand he rubbed his eyes.

Kupta watched with more than a passing interest. He took a generous sip of his brandy then said, "You've got to get some sleep before you drop. You're no good to anyone if you fall asleep at the helm."

Now Allen chuckled, his mood shifting. "I thought that's why I paid a certain navigator named Milton."

Kupta joined Allen in quiet laughter as he poured Hanson another glass of brandy then topped up his own half empty glass.

The atmosphere in the room was brighter than it had been only moments before.

"What do you plan to do, captain?" Kupta asked his face reverting to a grim expression.

Allen gazed hard into Kupta's eyes and said, "I'm going to pressure Milo Smyth to reassign her back to the Earth's Daughter."

"And how in heavens name do you propose to do that? I mean you can't go threatening to blow holes in him, or try that poker-bluff maneuver again.

Milo Smyth's no fool and he out ranks you."

Allen nodded and took a tentative sip of the fragrant brandy "Milo and I go back to the academy together." Allen shrugged. "I'm going to appeal to his sense of fair play. If there's one thing I know about Milo he's a fair man, and he knows that a star ship runs as much on its leadership as it does on its stomach."

Kupta frowned. "So you're expecting this desk jockey to understand that your crew is about to lynch you if you don't by some miracle get him to reassign Kelly Amstead?"

Allen smiled weakly and nodded. Kupta was about to add something when they were interrupted by another communication whistle. It was Bell's voice that came over the speaker next Allen's private viewer. "Bridge to Captain Allen."

Allen glanced at Kupta and cast the doctor a thin smile, as if to say they'd been saved by the bell from a knock down drag out argument.

"Do you want me to leave?" asked Kupta.

Allen shook his head and hit the white com button next to the speaker with his thumb. "Allen here."

"Captain, I have Admiral Smyth on viewer for you, sir."

"Put him through to my viewer, Lieutenant."

"Aye, sir." One of Allen's eyebrows went up his forehead, his eyes remained fixed on the doctors. The disappointment that the communication would be private was very evident in Bell's voice.

Allen hit the com button again to cut off his communication officer as the viewer on his desk shimmered and the image of Admiral Milo Smyth appeared.

Smyth's gentle brown eyes smiled warmly when he saw Allen. "Hanson. I received your message. You communications officer said it was urgent. Something about a planet-wide disaster?"

Allen glanced at Kupta and winced. He'd have to have a long talk with a certain lieutenant about message priorities.

Allen looked back at Smyth his expression changing to a sheepish grin. "Sorry, Milo, I think my crew may be getting a little space happy."

Smyth chuckled. "No problem, Hanson, I'm certain you'll ensure it never happens again."

Allen cringed inside. A fine way to start with me about to make demands, he thought.

Allen sighed. "Yes, sir. " Allen paused to gather his thoughts and his expression became hard. "The real reason I called is to discuss the transfer of one of my staff."

Milo looked surprised. "Oh?"

"Yeoman Kelly Amstead was transferred two days ago and is headed back to Earth. I agree with elimination of the captain's Yeoman program but—"

"Hold on, Hanson," said Smyth. "I would have expected your first officer to have briefed you by now."

Now it was Allen's turn to look surprised. Kupta frowned and the expression on his face said he was boiling inside, but he managed to remain silent even though it was obviously a struggle.

"Miller hasn't said anything…"

"As you know, Hanson, all crew assignments are done…"

"Through the first officer…yes, I know, Milo. Do you happen to know why she was transferred?"

"You should discuss that with your first officer. Smyth out." The viewer went dark.

Kupta burst before Allen could say anything. "Why didn't he tell you? Damn it, he knows the crew's upset. That scheming bastard has always been after the top job. He's trying to make you look bad. I otta …"

"Enough, Doc." Allen cut off the doctor with a warning glance then hit the com button again. "Allen to Miller."

Allen knew Miller was seated in the captain's chair on the bridge so he answered the hail immediately. "Miller here, sir."

"Report to my quarters immediately."

"Aye, sir, I am on my way." As usual the first officer's voice contained its standard issue calm.

With a few minutes the door to Allen's quarters opened and the blue shirted figure of Commander Bart Miller came in, his hands clasped behind his back. His coal black eyes and steely gaze met Allen's as he moved to stand beside the desk.

"Why don't you join us, Miller?" said Kupta raising his half filled glass of brandy in a toast, his gravely voice heavy with sarcasm.

"As you well know, doctor, I do not imbibe alcohol." Miller wasn't his real name. He was born on Regilus One and joined the fleet as an exobiologist sixteen years ago.

Since his race is known for a naturally calm manner he was nominated for command school at the academy, and had climbed the ranks ever since.

He'd been second in command of the *Earth's Daughter* for five years. Allen had been captain for three of those years

"Knock it off you two," said Allen. "Sit down."

Allen nodded to the other empty chair across the desk from the doctor.

Miller did as directed and sat down with his hands folded in his lap.

"Explain," said Allen his voice even.

"Sir?" said Miller.

"You know what he means, Miller," said Kupta.

A lone dark eyebrow over Miller's right eye rose up his pale forehead. "If you are referring to Kelly Amstead then I am unable to explain."

Allen couldn't believe his ears. It was as if his first officer had been expecting this line of inquiry. "That's an order, Mr. Miller." For the first time since he'd assumed command of the *Earth's Daughter* from Norm Kilani he was second guessing himself about his decision to keep Miller as his first officer.

At the time Norm told him Miller was the finest second in command in the fleet. With this latest turn of events Allen now had his doubts.

"I am unable to follow that order. Sir."

Allen snorted in frustration his eyes narrowing. "Well then at least tell me why."

"I am unable…"

"For pity's sake, Miller, you have to tell us something!" Kupta's voice swelled with anger as he stood up.

The veins in his forehead pulsed and his eyes bored through the stoic officer who sat unyielding gazing blandly at the ships doctor.

Miller crossed his arms over his narrow chest and said, "Doctor, there is no need for such emotional outbursts," he said, his thick voice as dry as the Mojave Desert.

Kupta turned to face Allen using his hands as wands to emphasize his point. "I'm telling you, Hanson, there's no reasoning with the man. He just doesn't get it."

"Doctor, as you yourself have pointed out on numerous occasions I am not a man, and I assure you I do *get it*."

Allen watched the interaction between his two senior officers with a half smile on his lips. "Okay, gentlemen I think that's enough. Doc, sit down."

Kupta reluctantly sat in his chair again, a look of frustration on his pale face. He stared at the first officer his eyes burning with pent up emotion.

Allen frowned. "I gather someone has solicited a promise from you not to tell me why Amstead was transferred. Naturally, as a Regilusian you must honor this request and keep this information even from me, your commanding officer. Am I correct, Mr. Miller?"

"You are, sir," said Miller.

Allen nodded slowly and studied the science officer's narrow features. "So given that you cannot tell me why Yeoman Amstead was transferred, Mr. Miller I suggest Yeoman Amstead herself requested the transfer."

Kupta's expression changed to shock. "What? Now Hanson I'm sorry but that doesn't make sense. Why would Kelly leave her friends without saying anything?"

"I don't know, Doc, but I plan to find out." Miller's cool eyes watched Allen as he again hit the com button.

"Bell, hail the *Wilson's Folly* and give Captain Jones my warm regards." Jones was an old freighter captain with heavy jowls, and a taste for brandy that rivaled Dr. Kupta's. But Strom Jones was also a man with scruples beyond question.

The red-cheeked image of Strom Jones shimmered to life on Allen's viewer. His appearance suggested he'd just enjoyed a taste from his brandy supply. A freighter traveling at level two star driver was more like a pleasure cruise. For the odd passenger they carried it pretty much was just that.

"Hello, Strom, it's Hanson Allen." Allen smiled warmly at the man with the fringe of gray hair that ran around his bald cranium like a halo.

Strom's wide face broke into a white toothy smile. "Hanson Allen, while I live and breathe. To what do I owe the honor of this call?"

"I was wondering if you still had that passenger aboard you picked up at space station Alpha 7, a blonde woman, mid-twenties."

Strom's suggestive chuckle made Allen wince inside but outwardly he remained the very image of friendly warmth. "Oh, yes that beauty is still aboard. She's been in her cabin for the last two days. Headed for Earth she says. Why Hanson?"

"I need to speak with her."

Strom shook his massive head. "Sorry, Hanson, but she left strict instructions not to be disturbed for the duration of the voyage. I don't ever violate a client's privacy, not for anyone. Not even a mighty ship captain like yourself."

Allen knew it was useless to argue with Strom so he decided to let it go, for now. He shrugged and said, "I understand, my friend. If at some point she comes out of her cabin will you inform her I wish to speak with her?"

Strom nodded with a brief smile on his lips. "Of course. Jones out." The viewer went dark instantly, almost as dark as Allen's mood.

He was getting nowhere fast. His first officer refused to divulge what he knew, and now Amstead refused to speak with anyone.

What was so damn secret? A cloud of remorse seemed to hang in the air. Maybe she'd left because… no, that couldn't be it.

\*\*\*

Two hours later Allen's eyes fluttered open his slumber interrupted by the communication whistle once again, and a soft voice bringing him once again into the world of the living.

Kupta had been right he did need sleep. His body felt as if it weighed twice its normal weight as he managed to sit up on his bunk and drop his lean legs over the side.

He rubbed his eyes to clear his bleary vision and then stepped onto the carpet and padded over to his desk. He punched the com button with his thumb.

"Allen here."

"Sir, I have Yeoman Amstead for you."

The weariness in his body left him and he felt more alert than he'd felt in days. *Kelly*? "Thank you, lieutenant, put her through."

The viewer shimmered and the image of Kelly Amstead appeared on the viewer screen.

She wore her hair loose about her shoulders the blonde hair, the color of shimmering straw, cascaded over her purple uniform jumper. Her blue eyes sparkled when she saw him and a brief smile crossed her lips.

"Captain," she said her voice bright and cheery.

"Yeoman Amstead, I'm so glad you called me back. We have something we need to discuss."

She lowered her eyes and her ivory cheeks flushed red. "Yes, sir. I'm very sorry to have caused you any trouble. I just didn't think…"

"That's what I'm afraid of, yeoman. You should have thought this through a little more before you just up and left my ship." Allen struggled to keep the bitterness from his voice.

Her eyes again made contact with his. "Yes, sir, you're quite correct. I told Mr. Miller, and I made him promise not to tell anyone…. I'm embarrassed….sir."

Allen's features registered his surprise. "Embarrassed about what, Kel…yeoman?" Allen felt the heat rising in his cheeks now.

"Well, sir, it's kind of a surprise. I plan to go back to the academy and study to be a communications specialist." Kelly's voice rose in excitement as she spoke.

"Bell and I have been talking about my finding a field of expertise for some time, and when the captain's yeoman program was canceled

I thought the timing was a sign for me to take the leap."

She smiled briefly then dropped her eyes to the floor.

Allen felt his heart sink. How could he have been so blind? This wasn't about him at all. It was about Kelly and her career.

"And when did you plan to tell the crew of my ship?" said Allen.

"When I was accepted into the program," said Amstead.

Allen nodded slowly. "Well, yeoman, then you did the right thing." Allen frowned. "Would it be alright if I told the crew, before you get to the academy? I would, of course send along my recommendations to the acceptance board."

Kelly smiled, her pearl white teeth showing and her eyes sparkled. "Yes, sir, that would be wonderful. I know I've upset everyone there. I'm truly sorry."

Allen sighed. "It's alright, Amstead. I'll handle things at this end."

"And, sir, I just want to say it was a real honor serving with you."

Allen smiled. "Amstead out." The viewer went dark before he could say anything more.

Allen thumbed the communication button. "Allen to bridge."

"Bell here, sir," came the immediate reply. Bell's finger must've been hovering over the switch for his com. He smiled to himself.

"Bell, I'm going to have a shower and a shave then I'll be up. Tell the crew that I'll be making a ship wide announcement when I arrive."

"Yes, sir."

*\*\**

Feeling refreshed after his nap, and the shower and shave, and dressed his usual uniform tunic, Hanson Allen walked onto the bridge of the *Earth's Daughter* feeling like a new man.

Miller immediately vacated the center chair and moved to his usual seat at the science station. Allen walked to his chair feeling the eyes of the bridge crew on him as he sat down.

He paused to offer a glance to Bell. He nodded his head slightly and she smiled back.

He then turned and faced the forward viewer and the blackness of star specked space that lay before them.

Allen hit the com button on his chair arm. He'd been thinking about what to say while he was in the shower and then while he shaved.

"Captain to crew. As you know Yeoman Amstead was transferred off this ship a few days ago. Amstead is a good friend to many of you and her sudden departure I know has caused concern among many of you." Allen paused.

"Yeoman Amstead has enrolled in Fleet Academy to become a communications specialist. She did this of her own volition and I can assure all of you her departure was not out of disrespect or malice toward this crew. In fact, she has assured me she was embarrassed to have caused any such feelings."

Allen swiveled his chair to lock eyes with his dark skinned communications officer.

"Kelly wishes me to pass along that it was an honor serving with you all, and that she hopes to serve with many of you again in the future. Captain out."

Allen saw the mist gather at the edges of Bell's eyes until she finally turned away to face her com board.

Just then Kupta walked through the lift doors and hurried to stand beside his chair. His voice was a whisper as he said, "Did she really say all that?"

Allen smiled and nodded. Suddenly he felt a presence beside him and Miller was standing beside his chair opposite doctor Kupta. His thin arms were locked behind his back. Kupta frowned and glared at Miller.

"This is your fault, Miller. You should have told us." Kupta pointed one finger at the Regilusian. Miller's right eyebrow climbed his forehead.

"As you know, doctor, that would have been impossible."

"Well, that's where you people could learn a few things from humanity…." Kupta fumed and blustered as he launched into one his vain attempts to humanize the Regilusian officer.

Allen smiled as he watched his two senior officers in their verbal tussle. He'd let them go on for a while this time.

He thought about Kelly Amstead and her secret. She was a fine person…a fine woman.

He had secrets of his own, which he wasn't about to share with anyone. Not even his two most valued friends in the universe.

# The Family Line

SEPTEMBER 15, 2389 IN ORBIT AROUND TELUS II

Paul Bellamo sat in the darkness his cabin aboard the Explorer Ship *Nastrodomo*. His skin was cold as ice, and his heart beat rapidly in his chest.

They were gone forever. And nothing would ever bring them back. He stroked the family photo album gently with the long fingers of his right hand. Theirs was a famous line that extended across the centuries making a difference.

It was so unfair.

OCTOBER 21, 1805 OFF THE SOUTHWEST COAST OF SPAIN, JUST WEST OF CAPE TRAFALGAR

Raul Bellamo stood on the sloping forecastle of the French first rate *Redoubtable* struggling to maintain his balance. His eyes and throat stung from the thick, acrid smoke that swirled about him. His once splendid blue uniform was dark with sweat, soot and blood.

His clean-shaven pale face was marred with his own blood, owing to the shrapnel that had so recently grazed his left ear.

In his left hand he held his saber at the ready, while a primed musket was gripped in his right. Intense sky blue eyes bled with tears due to the acrid smoke as he attempted to orient himself for the inevitable onslaught of the English marines. They were certainly somewhere within the thick cloud of swirling smoke.

*Redoubtable*, the pride of the French fleet had been slowed by a full barrage of the one hundred twelve cannons launched at them from Admiral Nelson's flagship, HMS *Victory*. Her sails shredded, her hull pocketed with cannon balls, the once mighty three-decked French vessel threatened to wallow, capsize and sink below the heaving seas off Trafalgar.

Bellamo was a junior officer on this, Admiral Villenuve's flagship. He realized now that the effort to break free of the English blockade had been seriously stymied. The Emperor's plan was lost.

Unlike the professionals of the French fleet their Spanish allies were reluctant sailors. It was doubtful the press gang crews of the Spanish fleet would be much use against the seasoned veterans of the English navy.

Bellamo stumbled across the deck as he wiped the tears that fogged his vision with the sleeve of his uniform tunic. He climbed the short grouping of four stairs that led to the quarterdeck from the now badly listing main deck. The ship creaked loudly in his ears.

"I hope she holds together," he murmured, as he stepped over fallen seamen, some with missing arms or legs.

Parts of the oak deck were slick with blood so he had to weave his way through his fallen shipmates without falling. He'd seen so much death in his short life that the grisly scene had little affect on him. Instead the sight of the dead or dying sailors only incited a heightened sense of rage deep within his belly.

Moans of the dying men echoed through the blanket of dark fog that was like a funeral shroud for the once mighty French fleet.

Finally, the black-gray smoke cleared enough for Bellamo to see the white-capped sea beyond. There, with flags waving in the breeze, its tall sails full with wind, its bow rising and falling as it split the green waters of the bay with white foam, was the pride of the English navy bearing down on their crippled vessel now heavy with excess water.

Bellamo knew they were about to be boarded, and unless he could locate some able bodied men to repel the enemy the ship was lost.

He looked around until he spotted, Robby, the ships mate, lying beside a water barrel. His eyes were open but the man was staring at infinity. The left side of his narrow face was covered with dried blood, his white beard peppered with bloody splatter.

Bellamo shook his head at the pitiful site of his old friend lost to him forever.

He moved to the aft section of the deck until the found a nest of wounded seamen. They were alive, huddled in small groups, their arms and legs tied with makeshift tourniquets. Good, this meant the ships surgeon was still alive.

He quickly located Dr. Gillespie who frantically moved amongst the wounded men tending as best he could to their traumatic wounds. Bellamo slipped the musket into the waistband of his trousers, and then replaced his saber in the scabbard dangling from the left side of his waist.

"Doctor, I need your help." Bellamo's voice sounded scratchy in his own ears. No doubt dry due to the smoke he'd inhaled.

Dr. Gillespie turned to gaze at Bellamo with hollow hazel eyes and a bland expression on his grime smudged features. His shoulder length blond hair, streaked with gray, which was normally tied in a neat ponytail, flew about his wide head in a nest of stray fibers. He acknowledged the junior officer with a slight nod of his head, and a heavy sigh. The sound sent a shudder through Bellamo. It was the most world-weary noise he'd ever heard.

The doctor stood slowly and Bellamo saw he held a dark stained wooden bowl filled with bloody water. His torn white shirt was also stained with dark red blotches.

"Mister Bellamo, there is very little I can do for you or anyone else on this ship."

"I need men. We are about to be boarded…"

The surgeon's eyes narrowed and his full lips became a terse line. "Then perhaps we should raise the white flag. We're in no shape to fight. And the captain is dead."

Bellamo's heart sank with this news. The Admiral….?

"And what of Admiral Villeneuve?"

Gillespie shook his head. "Alive. Barely. Sharp shooters."

Bellamo knew ships on both sides carried sharp shooters who perched in the ships rigging. Their orders were to decapitate the officers of an enemy vessel in order to leave them leaderless. He knew he was now in charge. And with a British ship of the line in full battle sail bearing down on them he also knew he had only minutes to mount a defense.

"Come with me, Doctor," he said briskly his tone and intense gaze daring the older man to refuse his order. The doctor nodded and followed as they headed for the quarterdeck where the ships wheel stood. The smoke was much lighter here so the sun washed blue sky was again visible.

Black tipped gulls cried overhead as they swooped and dived seemingly oblivious to the deadly battle taking place on the seas beneath them.

The odor of smoke cleared Bellamo's lungs to be replaced by the familiar smells of the sea, wind and salt that had first enticed him to join the navy.

When the two men reached the ships wheel Bellamo saw the dark skinned sailor, who he'd last seen steering the massive war ship, hanging limply from the spokes of the ships wheel. Bellamo rushed to the man's side only to see that the back of his skull was missing, having been blown away by an iron ball.

Without hesitation Bellamo pushed the corpse to the deck then turned to face the ships doctor.

"You will steer us away from that ship." He nodded toward the three massed English ship that rode the waves speeding toward them.

The doctor's eyes went wide with fear and his face paled as he spotted the English Navy ensign fluttering from the mast. The ship was very near now, and they could clearly see the red coats of the marines their muskets at the ready eager to board the helpless French vessel.

Bellamo glanced upward to the heavy rigging of the *Redoubtable* and spotted two sharp shooters hanging from the rigging, their muskets pointed at the officers gathered on the English fore castle. They were almost in range.

The English will pay for the deaths they've caused.

His breath caught in his throat and his mouth dried as he recognized one British officer's regal bearing. The man was an important target that he hoped the French sharp shooters would also recognize.

He looked around for anything that might help them thwart the enemy, while Dr. Gillespie took control of the ships wheel.

Bellamo felt the deck move beneath his feet as Gillespie spun hard in an attempt to steer their vessel away of the onrushing enemy ship.

Finally he spotted the stubby cannonade strapped in place with heavy twisted rope set below the horseshoe shaped rail at the rear of the dunette above him. A dead crewman lay on the deck below the gun; the still smoldering wick in his left hand had left its mark on the wooden planks.

Bellamo allowed himself a small smile and rushed up the short flight of steps to the gun.

He checked and sure enough it was primed, loaded and ready to fire. He glanced down at the dead sailor and silently thanked the man for saving the ship.

A glowing steel pot sat in the deck against the bottom rail where the wicks were kept to fire the guns. He picked one, then adjusted the gun to aim at the bow of the enemy ship as she swept toward them pushing boiling white foam ahead of her.

Just as it appeared they would catch the slower French vessel Bellamo fired. The shot was loud and a round iron ball flew from the barrel. It struck where the English marines stood and scattered them like wheat before the scythe.

Bellamo could see the English officers behind them begin to shout orders, and the one who was Bellamo's intended target moved quickly forward exposing himself to the French sharp shooters.

Bellamo heard a crack of a musket being fired from somewhere over his head followed by the report of another that echoed from the direction of the English vessel.

Bellamo felt a sudden, painful blow to his chest that pushed him backward and he fell to the deck.

He heard the doctor cry out as the surgeon rushed to his side. Bellamo's mouth filled with the taste of coppery blood. The doctor managed to lift him with one arm behind his back.

Bellamo felt weak and suddenly very cold. "Did we get him?"

"Who?"

"Nelson…" His eyes glazed over and the sunlit world began to slip into a deep, dark abyss.

"Yes. We got him," said the doctor, unsure in fact if this were true.

A soft smile crossed Bellamo's pained features. With one hand he managed to motion for the doctor to move closer to his lips. "Tell Marie and my precious Emil I love them…" he whispered.

His eyes closed and his body went limp. His last thought as the blackness took him was that the Bellamo family line would continue.


January 5, 2036 Stockholm, Sweden

Dr. Jean Bellamo gazed at the message dumbfounded. How could this be? Dr. Sloan's life threatened? That didn't make sense.

"No, this has to be a mistake." He shook his head to emphasize his point. His mouth was suddenly dry as if the coffee he'd just had had taken every ounce of moisture with it. He removed his wire-rimmed spectacles from his hawk like nose and rubbed his pale blue eyes with long craggy fingers.

"Dr. Sloan is a physicist not a politician. Why would anyone want to harm him?" Bellamo opened his eyes and stared at the round face of the bald headed Swedish police detective. The detective's cool blue eyes gazed back at him.

Detective Olafsson was only doing his job, but it was all such nonsense. No sane person threatens the life of a scientist. Not on the eve of the Nobel Prize presentations, unless….. A thought crossed his mind and his eyes hardened.

"I thought we were rid of those damned warlords," he said his voice tainted with deep strain of contempt. It was generally believed those power-mad genetic experiments gone awry had been purged from the surface of the planet over two decades ago. At least that's what most people believed. Bellamo wasn't so sure. Millions had died to rid the world of that corruption of science.

Maybe some of their fanatical followers were attempting to revive those dark times. After all Dr. Sloan's phase technology would make war a kinder, gentler pursuit and there were some fanatics who didn't wish the status quo to be disturbed. Sloan's genius would create a benevolent technology that would end bloody, painful death was not natural they argued. Ignorance was still humankind's chief curse.

"We don't know who's behind this, Dr. Bellamo," said Olafsson with a shrug of his wide shoulders. "We've tested the note in every way we can think of and nothing. We were hoping you might be able to tell us something. How long have you known Dr. Sloan?"

Bellamo smirked. "Albert and I worked together at Berkley." Bellamo placed the note on the faux pine hotel room table as he sat down heavily in the faux leather chair next to the table.

Olafsson sat across from him his sky blue eyes intent on Bellamo's every word. "Not exactly together mind you. Albert worked on his physics projects while I'm a chemist."

Olafsson nodded silently as he pulled out his data pad and placed it flat on the table with a barely audible click. He keyed as he asked questions and carefully record each response. Bellamo was impressed. Bright man this police officer.

"What are you receiving your award for, doctor? If I may ask."

Bellamo smiled and his eyes sparkled. "Transparent steel." The detective gazed at him with one eyebrow going slightly upward. Bellamo chuckled.

"It's based upon a formula I received from a glass manufacturer in New York some years ago. The man who gave it to me said he'd tried to make it work, but had been unsuccessful. He said two Scottish engineers sold him the formula for sheets of glass." Bellamo smirked. "Not that I believed him naturally. Many of these engineer types attempt new formulas using diverted funds from within their own company. This one failed to produce viable results so he gave it to me."

Bellamo paused again and regarded the detective with a stern expression. "What does any of this have to do with the threat to Albert?"

Olafsson shook his head and shrugged. "Nothing really. It's just that most suspects are often nervous and tend to be closed mouthed when ever I come along."

Bellamo eased back in his chair and unconsciously folded one long leg over the other. "I don't know whether to treat that as a compliment or be frightened to death."

It was the detective's turn to laugh.

"Sorry, doctor. It's just that we need to interview everyone attending the awards tomorrow and I've just eliminated you from my suspects list." Olafsson slipped his data pad into the inside pocket of his gray suit jacket. "Is there anything else you'd like to add before I leave you?"

"Do you know a restaurant nearby that serves good scampi?"

After the detective had left, not without suggesting the hotel's restaurant for dinner, saying it was the finest in Stockholm; Bellamo stepped into the adjoining bedroom in his suite to dress for dinner.

As was his habit he donned his tanned cotton golf slacks and a canary yellow open necked casual shirt. He slipped into his brown leather slip-ons to finish his ensemble for the evening.

The Royale's casino was supposed to be very good, or so some of his associates had told him on the flight from America. Not that he gambled a great deal but he did so enjoy the mental gymnastics inherent in a good game of poker.

As he left his room he swiped the lock with the card they'd given him when he'd checked in earlier in the day then set the voice-activated lock. The card would enable the main system at the front desk to keep track of who and how often the room was entered. The voice lock meant only he could enter the room other than hotel staff that needed to. Ever since the Ripson murders five years ago hotel security was a high priority. He shook his head sadly every time he thought about those poor women killed while they slept.

He walked the short carpeted hallway until he reached the bank of elevators.

One arrived within a few seconds of his pressing the down button. The doors opened and he was surprised to see Albert Sloan's smiling face staring back at him.

"Albert! What a pleasant surprise," Bellamo said as he entered. The elevator doors slid shut behind him and immediately began to move downward. Though there was very little sensation of movement within the car.

Bellamo gripped Albert's ebony hand in his and shook it warmly. For his part Albert placed one hand behind Bellamo's back as they shook hands.

"Peter," said Sloan (Albert always used the American pronunciation of Bellamo's name rather than the French. It was a private joke between the two men.) "It's nice to see you too. Where're you headed?"

"Thought I might try a little lady luck then catch a bite to eat. You?"

Albert chuckled as the let go of Bellamo's hand. "As I recall, Peter, you play a mean hand of poker." Bellamo grinned and nodded.

"Me? I love the slots. Doris and I used to make our yearly trek to Vegas just to play 'em."

Doris Sloan had passed away a year after being diagnosed with cancer. She'd been Albert's wife and best friend for over forty years. Too bad she hadn't lived to see his greatest success.

Bellamo had lost his wife at about the same time in a car accident.

The two men had many things in common except Albert and Doris had never had any children while he and Simone had two sons and a daughter. Unlike the Sloan's the Bellamo family line would continue.

"You want to meet for dinner in a couple of hours?" said Bellamo.

Albert nodded as the car arrived at the lobby level and the doors opened.

The two men parted company with grins on their faces each headed to a different part of the casino complex.

At exactly two hours Bellamo asked the dealer to cash him out as he rose from the card table. Poor Mr. Shipley to his left looked positively ecstatic that Bellamo was leaving.

Of course, Mr. Shipley's stack of chips was considerably reduced in the second hour of Bellamo being at this table. Little did Mr. Shipley know that he'd been up against one of the keenest poker minds of the twenty-first century. Bellamo had seen Mr. Shipley's tells after three hands and had waited to lay his trap in the last two hands.

He'd managed to make a few dollars and felt generally pleased with this evening thus far.

He took the chips to the cashier window and afterward headed for the slots to find Albert.

He strolled past machines with names like Brain Surgeon, Rocket Scientist, and Math Genius. Obviously casino management had recently changed their lineup of slots because these slot machines were supposedly designed to appeal to the Nobel Prize candidates staying at the hotel.

Bellamo smirked. Inane, positively inane.

As he rounded a bank of machines he spotted Albert his gazed fixed on the row of numbers on one of the math based dollar slots.

Bellamo glanced around and saw a man who looked out of place. He wore Bermuda shorts and a straw hat. Not one of those wide brimmed ones, but one of the fedora types. Dark sunglasses covered his eyes and he seemed focused on Albert's back as he walked briskly toward the physicist.

Bellamo felt a rush of adrenalin as he realized immediately something was very wrong. It all seemed like some slow motion movie as the man drew nearer to Albert he reached behind him and drew a pistol from the small of his back hidden underneath the gaudy orange and red Hawaiian shirt he wore.

Bellamo increased his pace until he was running with arms flailing.

His shouts of alarm drowned out by the sounds of the slot machines ringing and the blending of voices that blocked every sound. He hadn't noticed until now that the casino was crowded with tourists.

"Gun!" he shouted as loud as he could. He felt his heart pounding against his chest and his mouth was dry now as fear gripped him.

The man kept moving toward Albert his sunglasses fixed on his intended target. He was almost in range as the barrel of the gun was slowly but surely coming up to level. Albert had seconds to live.

Bellamo picked up his pace until he was so close to the killer he imagined he could smell his cheap aftershave. To cover the last leg of his journey Bellamo left his feet like a runner sliding for home. Just as the killer's gun came level Bellamo hit him in a full body tackle his arms wide as he gripped the stout man about his mid section.

Air rushed from both their lungs as he hit the man and then they were both on the gray and blue carpet of the casino. Bellamo felt a twinge of pain in his lower back as he wrestled with the gunman.

Suddenly there was a loud bang. Then another.

The would-be killers sunglasses had fallen off in the struggle and Bellamo could see the surprise that registered in his brown eyes.

The man jerked then went limp in his arms and Bellamo took procession of the gun.

He heard a voice say, "Drop it."

Bellamo let go of the gun, which fell to the carpet with a dull thud.

"Well, well if it isn't, Dr. Bellamo."

Bellamo glanced over his shoulder and saw Detective Olafsson with a wide grin pasted to his face, his service revolver out stretched in his hands aimed at the gunman who lay face down on the rug. There was a growing pool of blood that reeked of iron as the life drained from the would-be killers body.

"Thanks for the help, doc. You distracted him long enough for me to get him. I guess there's a lot more to you than a Nobel Prize winning egg head."

Bellamo closed his eyes and rolled flat on his back his long, lean arms stretched out to his sides.

I guess so, he thought, and then promptly fainted.

July 7, 2189 Mars Dome No. 2

Henri Bellamo gazed at the digital photos with tired eyes. He sighed heavily and ran one pale hand over his smooth hairless scalp. Like his father before him he'd lost the majority of his hair before the age of thirty-five.

Seven dead women in seven days and him with no leads. Damn this was the worst case of mass murder in colonization history and he had nothing to go on.

Bellamo's job was to keep the peace in Mars Dome Three, the so-called Euro Dome. He was ill equipped to handle what had been happening over the past week. The rapidity of the murders, and the single mindedness of it all, caught him and his lone constable completely off guard.

When he'd accepted the job as Chief Constable the recruiter from the United Earth Space Agency told him the assignment would be a cakewalk. Sure the licensed brothels tended to work on the finest of legal tight ropes but they were legal.

Until this mess began Mars was a quiet post. A few drunken brawls and kids stealing gum. Nothing they couldn't handle.

Though the victims so far had all been brothel workers he still worried about Yvette and his son LaRue's safety.

The miners who worked the asteroid fields had all been located and interviewed. Still nothing. No leads of any kind. It was as if the killer were a ghost.

Henri shook his head to remove such superstitious nonsense from his mind. He lifted his cup of coffee to his lips and nearly gagged when he took a sip into his mouth and realized it had grown cold some time ago. He swallowed the milky, sweet mixture and winced.

He placed the cup on the surface of his transparent steel desk then punched the white com button on the communicator built into the surface of the desk. The light next to the com unit came on indicating the voice mechanism was on.

"Sylvie, is there fresh coffee out there?"

A lilting, slightly accented voice responded. "Oui, Henri." Sylvie was always in a good mood. His mood on the other hand was as dark and as foul as this coffee.

"Thank you." He thumbed the button again to close the link and the light winked out.

He rose from behind his desk and his muscles in his lean body protested his every move. His gray UESA uniform jumper felt tighter than usual. He decided he needed more exercise.

Martian gravity was different from Earth's, or so the doctors had warned him. When they'd arrived with the first colonists two years ago the medical corps cautioned them that daily exercise was needed to counter the loss of bone mass in a lower gravity environment such as Mars.

In a hundred years or so the planet wide re-engineering would make Mars more Earth normal. But until that time Martian residents needed to follow the strict regimes inherent in adapting to their new environment.

He moved across the carpeted floor of his office past the brown leather couch that sat against one wall and the potted palm sting next to it that he'd grown from seedlings brought from Earth. The doors to the outer office opened with a soft swoosh moving the recycled air as they parted to allow him to exit.

Sylvie sat smiling behind her desk as he entered the lobby her dark flowing curls and pale porcelain skin glowed with health. Her dark eyes were fixed on her boss. He crossed to the coffee machine to the left of where she sat and began to fix himself a fresh cup.

"You know, Henri you shouldn't put milk and sugar in your coffee. It's not good for you," she said.

Like his wife, Yvette the next thing she'd be suggesting is he drink that horrid Earl Grey she loved so much, instead of his beloved coffee.

As Bellamo lifted the cup toward his lips he said, "And you should always speak Earth standard in the office." He was of course referring to her use of French when she responded to his question over the intercom. The UESA preferred its employees to stick to Earth standard for all official duties.

Bellamo, his nostrils filled with the scent of sweet fresh coffee, turned to face his loyal assistant who wore a mischievous smile as flashing eyes met his gaze. He smiled in return then without saying another word walked back into his office the doors sliding shut behind him.

Once back behind his desk Bellamo hit the com button again. "Signal Blake I wish to see him in my office right away." Sylvie acknowledged his request then closed the link.

*Maybe I was a little hard on her.* He resolved he'd make it up to her later. Maybe buy her dinner.

Blake Noseworthy was Bellamo's second in command.

In fact Blake was his only command, but a good man and someone Bellamo trusted.

While he waited for Blake to arrive Bellamo again pulled up the crime scene reports and digi-photos. The vital clue had to be in here somewhere.

The UESA detectives and forensic specialists wouldn't arrive for another day. By that time he hoped to have something more for them that the wisps of smoke he'd managed to collect thus far.

The doors to his office swooshed open and the blond blue eyed giant with the square jaw of Blake Noseworthy rushed through the doors. He stopped in front of his boss' desk and stood casually his meaty hands at his sides.

"Yes sir?" he said in his characteristic deep voice.

Bellamo regarded Blake with one eyebrow raised. "Sit down, Blake."

Bellamo nodded to the forest green cloth covered chair that sat across the desk. Blake immediately sat down his eyes focused on Bellamo's. Since they'd began to work together the two men had become like brothers.

There were times Bellamo was certain Blake could actually read his thoughts.

"I have a plan," Bellamo began. "We're going to end this thing tonight."

Blake nodded grimly his eyes as hard as diamond and his jaw line tight.

* * *

Five hours later Sylvie sat shivering in a booth at Le Café, a coffee house across from the row of brothels that ran down Churchill Street in sector B, the area known as the red light district.

The place was deserted except for a greasy haired waiter, the cook in the back and Sylvie. She sat with a cup of Earl Grey in front of her keeping her coat pulled up around her neck. She cast a wary gaze on the street outside.

A few of the brothel workers were talking with some miners who'd just left one of the bars down the street.

Sylvie cringed inside. *How did I ever let Henri talk me into this? He said I'd be perfectly safe.* "Yeah right," she muttered.

"Yeah?" It was the oil-slick haired waiter with the fox like face and the beady eyes. He stood over her with an empty black plastic serving tray held aloft in his right hand.

"Sorry," she said. "I'm waiting for someone."

The waiter smirked. "Yeah, sure you are, lady."

111

He shrugged.

"If you need anything I'll be over at the counter watching the Wimbledon matches."

She nodded. "Okay, thanks." She smiled weakly. He grimaced and walked away leaving her alone once again.

She glanced at her digital watch and saw that it was time. The murders had all occurred at about the same time of night.

The street workers had been recruiting customers in the street when they disappeared.

The street hadn't been deserted each time there was a murder yet no one had seen anything. It was as if the victims just vanished.

The bodies turned up later in one of several streets that led to this area of the dome. The victims had been horribly mutilated and disemboweled.

As she stood in the dim light watching the pedestrian traffic go by some of the miners winked at her, but with the look she made it very clear she wasn't interested. Nothing more happened for some time.

"Where are you, Henri?" she whispered under her breath.

A familiar voice interrupted her thoughts. "Hello, Sylvie." It was Blake.

"Oh, Blake it's you." She whirled and faced the big man.

He grinned easily and wrapped his long muscular arms around her.

"You okay?" he said. "You're shivering."

"I think I've had enough for one night," she breathed as they parted. "I should never have told Henri I would do this. I'm scared out of my wits."

Blake nodded. "I understand. Can I walk you home?"

"Yes, please, if you don't mind?"

Blake nodded a grin on his face as he held out one arm. "Come along, my lady."

She giggled and a brief smile crossed her lips. "Ah, sir knight, such gallantry. I accept."

With a flourish that harkened back to the days of chivalry they walked arm in arm toward one of the streets that led them away from the sector B toward sector G where Sylvie resided.

Once sector B was behind them Sylvie relaxed and they walked along in silence for several seconds until Blake said, "You like the boss don't you?"

"Why whatever gave you that idea?" Sylvie could feel the heat rise in her face.

"Oh, I don't know. It could be the way you look at him, or the trace of drool that runs down your chin wherever you're around him."

She slapped his left arm playfully. "Oh, I do not."

"Yes, you do. You're in love with him aren't you?" He said it with enough conviction that it caused her to stop and turn to face him.

"If I was what business would it be of yours?" She surprised herself with the forcefulness of her response. She was angry.

He shrugged. "None, of course, it's just that…."
"What?"

"Well, if it's true I'm going to have to kill you."

Sylvie heart skipped a beat and her mouth went dry. "You're what?"

"Kill you," he repeated. He reached behind his back and pulled out a large curved blade that glistened in the low light of the artificial Martian dusk.

She stepped back, hands raised to a defensive position, a scream choked in her throat. She was too afraid to scream.

*This isn't right. Blake's one of the good guys.*

He moved with the reflexes of a cat and was swiftly upon her. She could smell the roast beef he'd had for dinner still lingering on his breath.

There was a slight pinch in her stomach as his meaty left hand pulled her slim body toward him and impaled her with the knife.

Suddenly her hearing was filled with the sound of a laser weapon being fired.

She felt Blake jerk against her then they fell as one with his full weight on top of her, the knife pressing deeper into her flesh.

Finally a gargled scream escaped her lips only to be muffled by his body as they hit the tiled floor of the street.

She couldn't breath. She was dying and she knew it.

Hands pulled Blake away from her and she could once again manage a breath. Her lungs burned. The pain from the knife was increasing. Her toes and fingers felt colder than they'd ever felt before. Not even Minnesota winters were this cold.

A familiar face bent over hers. Through foggy vision she recognized Henri's handsome features. "Sylvie, I'm so sorry. I had no idea…" His voice trailed off.

She managed to raise one weak hand to her lips to silence him then motioned for Bellamo to come closer. He bent over her one ear hovering above her bloodstained full lips.

"I love you, Henri Bellamo. I always have," she whispered.

Until she sagged and her eyes closed for the last time as the swirling dark vortex of death took her.

*** 

Henri Bellamo stood over his assistant's body his heart heavy with regret. She loved him so much she'd sacrificed her life to help him solve the murders.

He moved to Blake and checked for a pulse. Nothing. The man was dead.

Good riddance to him. How could he have been so wrong about him? Maybe he needed to give up this job and return to Earth. He certainly couldn't be a constable anymore, not with Sylvie's blood on his hands.

He resolved to one day tell young LaRue about this day. Maybe there was lesson in this for his son. Then again, maybe not.

Odd thing was the laser weapon had been set on stun not kill. Blake shouldn't be dead yet he was.

There were many odd things about all this. He shrugged his narrow shoulders. The investigators would get to the bottom of it, after all that was their job wasn't it?

A steel gray haired man with the cool dark eyes stood amongst the crowd that had gathered to see what was happening.

He gazed at the chief constable with a faint smile on his thin lips.

The man turned and walked away headed for the spaceport. It was time to move on.

September 15, 2389 in orbit around Telus II

The family line was at an end. His dearly beloved nephew, Robert was the last son of the Bellamo family. The last hope.

Paul recalled the stories papa had told him and his brother, Pierre as they sat round the campfire. The blanket of stars that washed the summer sky overhead had been a beacon to him even then. More so than having a family of his own. Pierre took care of the family line for them both. But the deadly fire had burned out the family line.

As boys he and his brother reveled in those tales of triumph and tragedy that papa had lain before them. Trafalgar, the Nobel Prize, the Martian colonies… the Bellamo line had been there throughout history. Humankind was better off for having Bellamo's.

Now that was over—

—there would be no more Bellamo family line.

# Big Business

He who's the fattest wins.

The banner running across the poster of the new triple cheesier was the company slogan fifteen-year-old Peter Pug really hated.

He gazed at the banner fluttering in the gentle breeze hung over the entry doors of the glass tower that ran up seventy stories into the white puffy clouds the weather bureau had created for today.

He paused his hover chair to scratch the roll of fat that hung over the left side of the gravity belt struggling to keep his silver stretch pants above his waist line. The goal was to live up to those important words. He had never felt capable of living up to his mother's expectations never mind the company motto.

The best burgers and fries made them the second largest fast food company in the galactic franchise wars.

Heavenly Sky Burger had somehow never been able to crack the glass ceiling to make it to number one.

Peter floated inside and took the high-speed elevator to the executive office on the seventh floor. He entered his mother's office to find her seat in her hover chair behind her expansive plasti-steel desk engrossed in something on her vid screen inset into the smooth desktop.

Without looking up she said, "There you are." Her voice was deep and throaty. "Where have you been?"

"Huh..I've been down in food additives supervising some new…"

"Forget that crap," she said interrupting with a wave of a bloated hand.

"Yesss, mother," he said, his voice trembled as fear ran through his gelatin like frame, which caused him to tremble and jiggle. She was a scary woman, like most people of absolute power. His father was the only person he'd ever known to stand up in the face of her intimidation, and won.

"I've a very important job for you, and this time you'd better not screw it up."

His eyes fixed on the thick pile of the purple and gray carpet that covered the flexi-steel floor of her office.

The delicious greasy smells coming from the insta-burger bar against the far wall made his stomach rumble. He hoped she'd let him eat soon.

"Com'on, Peter, let's get something to eat. I'll fill you in on the details." Her tone lightened.

The chair lifted away from the desk then carried her to the food bar by sliding on its four-wheeled base. It was the latest automatic model made for the obese woman who had everything. And Trixie Pug, as Chief Operating Officer of HSB, had everything.

The insta-burger deposited a triple cheeseburger with a large side of french fries on a white-coated metal platter and slid it to the edge of the counter. The smell made Peter's mouth water. He swallowed the extra saliva.

Trixie lifted it from the platter between her well-rounded digits.

Peter strode after her with a plate of the new fried chicken. He really wanted his usual burger, but what he wanted most was to please his mother, and she wanted him to try the new product. At least it was deep-fried. He stopped his hover chair across the desk from her.

She grimaced at him as she raised the burger to her ample mouth, tore a large bite off and began to chew loudly with her mouth open.

"Hummpf," she mumbled in between chews, "I have a mission for you. It involves your father."

He stopped in mid-bite of greasy chicken his mouth gapping at her. His father? Sure he was the best FTL scientist in the galaxy, and probably the most responsible for the continued expansion of the HSB, but he also knew his mother detested him.

He insisted on being slim and trim when normal people prided themselves on being as fat as humanly possible. Obesity is in and fat is beautiful, baby. Doctor of Engineering, Herman Pug voted the skinniest guy in the class of 3302 (not an honor) was the black sheep amongst the Pugs.

\*\*\*

Herman Pug studied the three dimensional schematic image of the engine hovering over his desk.

Yes, it just might work.

Trixie's quest for power and her efforts to become the number one fast food company were dangerous obsessions as far as he was concerned.

The love he'd once felt for her vanished with the gathering weight and the accompanying cravings for power that propelled her up the corporate ladder.

He recalled fondly the times she joined the HSB marketing department as a junior executive. They'd soon gone their separate ways when the love she'd felt for him was replaced with grease.

These days he put all his energy into his engines. Especially when he wasn't the one paying the bills.

Mickelott, the half moon shaped purple from Marzipan Two. A planet named by some dumb ass pilot from one of the two fast food giants. They were always naming newly discovered planets after some condiment. It made for some down right weird names; Olives, Ketchup and Double-Onions-Raw-or-Fried.

Mickey sat quietly on the edge of the table happily slurping on his bowl of green mush. Herman wondered why whoever decided such things hadn't called the aliens planet green mush.

"Mickey, do you really have to make all that noise? I'm trying to work."

The transparent purple slug's front end that Herman concluded long ago was his mouth was not his ass.

"Yeah, well you're interrupting my meal."

The little alien's words shot through his mind. God how he hated telepathy, but the little guy had grown on him ever since he'd found the alien stowed away on one of the automated marketeer FTL ships.

Herman had been a receiving clerk at the time and his duties included unloading marketeers returning from deep space marketing missions. He had discovered Mickey dehydrated and starving. After nursing him back health they'd become best friends forever.

The bell on the entrance door to the lab buzzed interrupting his train of thought.

"Come," he said. This single word caused the double doors, visible from his desk, to swoosh as they slid aside.

There stood his son, Peter in his silver gravity suit, his massive stomach sticking out in front of him. His cheeks seemed puffier than when he'd last seen him a year ago; no doubt he'd gained weight since then.

This was unexpected. Oh, now what? thought Herman.

Mickey's gossamer wings appeared from the sides of his body. They spread outward and began to flap, making him appear to be some purple alien bird. He lifted off and began to hover in place near the desk.

"Hi, Dad," said Peter. He glanced about his father's lab, his eyes nervous.

"I'm rather busy right now." Herman kept his gaze fixed on the image that rose off the glass surface of his desk. "Holo off."

The image vanished and he sat down heavily in the black executive leather chair behind it.

*\*\*\**

Peter saw Mickey move away until he hovered over the large air couch set against one wall. The dim light made it difficult to see him floating there.

Peter moved his hover chair purposefully toward the desk. (At least he hoped it appeared purposeful. You could never tell with a hover chair.)

Once he stopped he glanced about the room nervously. The odor of his own perspiration filled the room. Perspiration now flowed off his forehead in rivulets. He reached into a breast pocket of his suit to extract a white towel, which he used to wipe off the excess moisture. He hated when mom sent him down here to speak with dad. They really hated each other. It made him nervous.

"You should lose some weight," his father said with a deadpan expression.

"Yeah…right." Like that would ever happen. And if he did everyone'd ostracize him.

His father put his hands in the pockets of his white lab coat and eased back in his chair. "So what do you want?"

"Who says I want anything? Maybe I just dropped by to see my dear old dad?"

"Don't start with the bull, kid."

"Huh… yeah." Peter leaned forward, as much as he was able, his belly didn't allow him much movement. "Listen, could you ask that slug thingy to get out of here so we can talk."

"He's my trusted lab assistant actually, whatever you say to me you say to him."

Peter fidgeted visibly as he struggled with the next words out of his mouth. "Listen, Dad, this isn't easy…

"Your mother needs my help? Right?"

Peter's face flushed and his mouth hung open. His blood shot blue eyes went wide, like a space bug before it hit the windshield of a shuttlecraft. He stammered unable to speak.

"She wants my latest engine doesn't she?" His Dad crossed his arms across his chest a move which would have killed Peter had he attempted it. Not that he would ever try. "You can get you're fat butt back to her right now and tell her to forget it."

Peter struggled to his feet and fled his father's laboratory his hover chair's motor whining under the strain of the sudden increase in speed.

*** 

Herman could hear the echo of his son's labored breathing as the doors swooshed shut behind him.

"That was a little harsh don't you think?" said Mickey.

"They piss me off. They're all about greed. I'm a scientist damn it, not a profit monger. There's no way in hell I'm giving them another of my inventions. They'll waste it on some hair brained market expansion plan. I'm an explorer at heart."

Herman thought he could hear the little purple roll his eyes, if he'd had any eyes to roll. Mickey didn't approve of Herman's attitude toward his son.

They'd stayed up late at the nearby poker parlor many a night talking, arguing really, about Peter and his ex-wife. Mickey advocated involvement in his son's life.

Herman said he didn't want any part of the corporate life that Peter and Trixie whole-heartedly embraced.

He didn't care about being the fattest, or the greediest. It seemed to him money and fat, and fat and money was all they cared about. He wanted none of those things. As far as she was concerned their lives' were wasted.

To him it was sad and reprehensible at the same time.

Build them a newer and faster FTL ship? Trixie had been trying for years to get him to build her one. He frowned and crossed his arms over his chest. Never.

*\*\**

"What do you mean he won't help us? We own his ass."

Peter cowered before his mother. She floated her chair carrying her massive bulk to the food dispenser to order a triple cheese with fries.

He felt pride as he watched her move across the spacious office. She was good and fat. Through the window he watched as many as five automated FTL ships launch from the docking bay doors at once.

The leather over stuffed chair he sat in creaked as he tried to shrink into it. He wanted to disappear, a physical impossibility for a boy with a seventy-two inch waist.

"But, Mom…" He was cut short by her glare, her dark eyes bored through him over the sesame seed covered bun of the triple cheeser. His stomach growled as the delectable odor of the cooked meat and cheese wafted over him. He swallowed hard. "I tried…"

"Never mind," she said cutting him off with a fierce snap in her voice. The last bite of burger, secret sauce, and cheese disappeared as Trixie paused to steeple her enormous greasy fingers.

Her beady eyes narrowed. Her chewing was the only thing breaking the silence. "Tell him I want to see him. Tomorrow," she said, after the last large swallow of her burger.

She chuckled to herself. Her rolls of fat, beneath the green and red flowers of her muumuu, waved as if in a strong breeze. With a wave of her corpulent hands she dismissed him.

He struggled out of the chair and adjusted the gravity setting on his chair to retreat as fast as his massive body would allow.

As he neared the exit doors he heard her murmur to herself. "I need to meet with the board this afternoon."

Her sharp laugh followed him to the outer office to be cut off by the doors as they clapped shut with a loud thunk.

\*\*\*

At precisely nine the next morning Herman Pug, accompanied by Mickey who flew over his left shoulder, strode into the spacious office of Trixie Pug, President of Heavenly Sky Burger.

Her eyes narrowed as she saw him walk in with his purple slug. She'd turn on the old charm and set it to full.

Trixie's huge face contorted to be equal parts pleasure, apprehension and wariness. Then again it might just be gas. She was well aware her ex-husband didn't usually respond well to summons from her.

Perhaps her memo stating that the funding for his research was being reduced to zero percent had been the deciding factor after all. They both knew it was an empty threat but the game had to be played. They both knew that HSB needed R&D as much as it needed marketing if they were to remain competitive.

"So," she began then her voice trailed off.

He kept his hands in the pockets of his white lab coat. The awkward silence between them elongated and beads of perspiration began to appear on her forehead.

Framed by the window behind her were a number of auto-ships taking off and one small flitter its navigation lights glowing and blinking pulling a sign behind it. A string of glowing multicolored lights that blinked at regular intervals surrounded the sign. In the center of the sign were the words; He Who's the Fattest Wins.

He grimaced. A perplexed looked crossed Trixie's face until she glanced behind to see what he was looking at.

"You never approved of what we're trying to do." She said it in a matter of fact manner. Not as a question, but as a statement. He kept staring out the window.

"How can I?" he said. "You're killing the human race."

She spun her chair to face him and a flash of anger crossed features. Her puffy cheeks glowed red as if her skin were on fire. "We are advancing the corporate business plan. Big business is a reality. We're here to stay whether dissidents such as you like it or not."

Herman stiffened and he felt his hands tighten in the pockets of his lab coat. He spoke from between gritted teeth. "I didn't come here to have the same old argument with you, Trix. What do you want?"

Trixie regained her composure and adjusted her bulk in her chair. As she did so her face transformed into a smile, one that was politician like, presidential in a way. She was supposed to go corporate during times like this, and that was one area where she was particularly skilled.

Being the second best corporate president in the galaxy had taught her something, if in doubt bullshit.

"Let's not start off in the wrong direction. I have an offer for you."

"One that I can't refuse?" said Gary his voice dripping with sarcasm. Halo chuckled as he floated nearby thoroughly enjoying the action. He loved the interaction of humans. From the corner of his eye Herman looked at the purple and a brief smiled crossed his lips. He then returned a stoic gaze at Trixie.

She smiled broadly. "Of course you can refuse, but I think you will like what I have to offer."

A small control panel appeared from her desk and she pushed a button. A holo-screen dropped down from a five-foot slot in the ceiling. The overhead lighting system dimmed.

"Cool. Movies," said Mickey drifting over to the couch against the opposite wall. Herman remained in the chair in front of Trixie's desk.

"Where's the popcorn?" said the alien. Trixie glared at Herman who shrugged.

Trixie touched the control panel again and the red and blue Planet Burger logo appeared on the screen in living holo-color. The company theme song began to play again.

The scene immediately shifted to a picture of Trixie sitting behind her desk.

"Hello, I'm Trixie Pug, President of the Heavenly Sky Burger Corporation. I'm speaking to the board of directors today about our new improved corporate business plan, our most ambitious yet." Trixie's image paused for dramatic effect.

"No, it does not involve a new improved menu, as I'm sure we're all used to." Trixie chuckled, as did her likeness on the screen. "I love that joke," said Trixie.

Herman smirked and shook his head.

Trixie's image turned to the camera. "Shortly we will be opening exciting new markets. I'm speaking about a new class of FTL ship that will take us to the Andromeda galaxy. A place where no fast food company has gone before." The faux Trixie raised one meaty arm over her head and her face became bright red.

Her image was replaced by the HSB logo. An announcer's voice, a man who spoke in the style of a man being chased by mad dogs (which maybe he was), came over hidden speakers. "This program is copyrighted by the HSB Corporation. No part may be duplicated in part or in whole without the expression written permission of the company.

Failure to adhere to this strict company policy will result in an immediate death sentence without benefit of trial."

"And the fat lady sings," said Mickey cackling.

The lights came up as the widows once again became clear and the room returned to its original configuration.

Herman removed his hands from his pockets and placed them folded in his lap.

"So," he began slowly," I'll ask again what does any of this have to do with me?"

"Isn't it obvious?" said Trixie with a puzzled expression. Anyone could clearly see what they were getting at. Herman, however, shook his head.

"They want to have your new FTL drive. Or they go under," said Mickey who'd risen from the couch his wings spread from his purple slug shaped body allowed him to float as if on he was a butterfly on a gentle breeze.

Trixie pointed at the purple alien. "What he said." She eased back in her chair her arms at her sides a satisfied smiled across her ruddy complexion.

"What's in it for me?" said Herman.

He'd planned this moment for weeks. He knew it was only a matter of time before one of the fast food giants approached him for his know how.

He knew he could get his wife to make the best deal of the two biggies. Even though he currently worked for Planet Burger jumping ships wasn't unheard of, not in corporate culture where it was dog eat dog (he suppressed the urge to laugh at this thought).

He remembered 'ol Marty Smartman, the candy prize pack king, who'd started out in corporate development at Pizza Comet until he'd stolen all the patents for the toys in the kids packs, then set himself up as the exclusive supplier of toys to every fast food company in the known galaxy.

It was something Trix knew as well as he did, maybe even better. No, she wouldn't miss this opportunity. No siree.

He had his eye on a little paradise planet, near the relish worlds of Green Dill and Hamburger Red. This deal would finally give him the money to escape the corporate rat race, and maybe alleviate himself of some familial baggage at the same time.

All he needed to do was play his cards right.

Trixie piggy eyes narrowed until they were mere slits of dark matter. She placed her flabby arms flat on the polished surface of her desk. They spread out like two pools of steaming flesh colored goo.

"How about ten percent?" An eyebrow arched.

He gazed impassively into the slits above Trixie's bulbous cheeks. "Are you joking?"

She smiled. "Somehow I didn't think you'd roll that easy. Okay. What's reasonable?"

She eased back in her chair and gazed at the little purple hovering across the room, its web like wings flapping lazily in the still air.

Herman sensed the fear start deep in his stomach. Butterflies moved. He mentally pushed the feeling down. He smelled the grease coming from her pores. She was nervous, but didn't show it outwardly. It dawned on him that the corporation had a final offer in mind. He decided to go for broke.

"Fifty one percent of what ever profits are realized in the expansion to Andromeda."

Both eyebrows went up. "Since when you become so corporate?" She smiled. "Of course, we can't give you controlling interest." She didn't make a counter offer, so he did.

"I understand, how about five trillion in cash and stock options?" He kept his face free of any expression. This was what he really wanted. The cash would buy him a reliable ship, to get to his new planet, which he would buy, the real estate fees, taxes and with enough spending money left over to retire in comfort for the rest of his days.

"Okay," she said, "deal."

He realized he'd made it too easy, but he'd gotten what he wanted, and so had she.

\*\*\*

Mickey hovered over his shoulder as Herman watched the new FTL ship slip through the bay doors. Trix was nice enough to let him watch the launch from her office.

She told him skinnies weren't allowed on the VIP platform on the hangar deck. Only the beautiful people were allowed. Besides she said the wide-angle lenses would most certainly miss one skinny little guy amongst all that beauty.

The ship disappeared in a blinding burst of light as the new engine was engaged. They were on their way to disappear on a long journey.

He smiled.

"How long are they going to be gone?" said Mickey.

"A long time," said Herman as he reached into the pockets of his white lab coat and pulled out two round balls. These were the drive crystals that made the FTL system work. One set got you where you were going, while and another set got you back.

It was a small detail. One that he'd failed to share with Trixie, or Peter, when they insisted their executive assistants on going on the maiden trip.

He thought maybe they'd start a new fast food company over there? Who knows maybe the Andromeda's possessed their own fast food companies. You just never know. Big business was a harsh mistress. The fattest lost this time. The two assistants were never coming back. The trip was one way, a voyage of no return.

Trixie would have to honor their agreement or lose face to the board of directors. He'd proven the new technology. She just hadn't been specific enough. She never said the ship had to return.

Boy, was she going to be mad at me. He smiled to himself.

He walked away from the window with Mickey close behind. The doors opened and he walked out to begin his journey to his new home closer to the freedom he so craved.

# In Search of the Perfect Cup

TREVOR WATKINS SAT PRONE in front of his Mac his fingers poised over the keyboard staring at the empty page. The gray cursor at the left side of the screen flashed intermittently as if to urge his long, narrow fingers to write. Something anything. Instead, it reminded him of his failure. His advance was nearing depletion and he had nothing to show for it. At least very little his publisher would appreciate.

The only thing interrupting the silence in his study came from his extra large tumbler of cola. It popped and fizzed to its own drummer oblivious to his frustration. The air was filled with the odor of sweet cola.

In conducting his research, Trevor had traveled to every country and city on Earth to find the perfect cup.

Not in the Paris café's or the Istanbul coffee houses or the London bistro's or the finest New York restaurants or even in the Mall of America.

# In Search of the Perfect Cup

It seemed nowhere on God's blue Earth was the perfect cup to be found. He'd drunk so much swill that he was certain his blood had been replaced by black ooze. He was also sure he'd die of a coffee overdose before he finished. Either that or his editor would kill him. Of the two options open to him right now he preferred the latter. Wally would kill him for sure.

The editor of the largest publishing house in De Moines last e-mail had made Wally's intent plain. "Write or die" was as clear as anyone ever got about such things. And if he knew Wally Vesper as well as he did, he meant what he said.

You'd think after three successful coffee table books he should be able to write this one with ease. But he was stymied. And after all the project's he'd completed this one should be the easiest yet. It fulfilled his life-long dream. This was the reason he'd become a writer in the first place.

His hands dropped to his side then he leaned forward to rest his elbows on his pine work desk and eyed the screen as if it were his sworn enemy. Damn it, he'd interviewed thousands of people from every walk-of-life. Their eyes were lit by an inner passion when they told him where to find the perfect cup of the black elixir he called coffee.

Busmen, waiters, construction workers, office workers, celebrities, coffee company executives, CEO's, dishwashers, they all said the same thing, "It was the best cup I ever tasted." Unfortunately, none measured up.

Maybe what he's sought for so long didn't exist? But how could that be? He'd had one, once. The most perfect cup he'd ever tasted had been only the once.

It was so long ago he could just barely recall that heavenly flavor. Even today, when he closed his eyes he swore he could still taste the aromatic flavor of it when the coffee mingled with cream and sugar and danced over his taste buds.

It was the time when he was a kid that his Mom had made him what was to be her last cup of coffee. At the tender age of thirteen she'd said he was finally old enough to have his first cup. She died in her sleep that night and her coffee recipe died with her. He'd never a tasted a cup like it since.

Trevor was a junkie. Hooked on the bean, his wife Charlotte told her friends at the local beauty parlor. He agreed with her. Why deny it? He was hopelessly addicted, but there were worse things in life.

When he'd approached Wally with the idea he thought the cynical publisher would never buy it.

To his surprise, he loved the idea. Trevor recalled at the time how happy he'd been. He'd managed to blend his obsession with his work. What could be the more perfect match? Except, it hadn't worked out quite like he'd expected, had it?

With his eyes closed he hung his head; his long, gray-flecked hair covered his thin face. He buried his face in his hands shuddered then sat up and straightened himself in his chair. He needed to shake this mood off to get back to work. I'm a pro, he thought. Act like one.

His red-rimmed eyes focused on the screen in front of him. He wrinkled his nose. Ugh, he thought, I even smell bad to me. He paused to take a generous sip of the cola. The bubbles tickled his nose as the sweet soda went down his throat where it cooled his tongue and the inside of his mouth as it disappeared into his digestive tract.

Trevor pressed the button that would link him to the net. "Might as well," he muttered, "nothing else to do."

As usual the Internet opened up and took him to his own website. The flashy advertising of Starbucks and Coffee Express gyrated on the edges of his vision. The screen was now filled with the map that recorded his worldwide quest.

He glanced down and noted the tracker at the bottom right corner of the screen now showed over one hundred thousand hits. Not great but not bad either.

He consoled himself with the thought that if he ever managed to complete the book some of the people who took time to follow his travels might even buy it.

Something caught his eye. He stared in awe as his jaw hung loose. There. On the Oregon Coast... there's something different. He moved the cursor over the pacific coast and drilled down using the spyglass feature until he was at street level.

He focused on the area south of Lincoln City. Odd. There's a new dot on the map. Very tiny. Almost too small to see with the naked eye. It's a town he'd never seen before at that location. Between Nelscott and Taft. A place called Almost. Almost, Oregon?

A shiver of excitement ran through his body. Maybe it's a sign? He opened his favorites list and Googled the name. Almost Oregon. The list showed ten billion hits. The first site listed was the town's website. He moved the cursor over the website and clicked it.

There wasn't much. Population six. Located on Highway 101 between Nelscott and Taft. Total area ten acres. One business. "Hmmm...Le Petite Café...The Little Café?" Trevor rubbed his gray streaked goatee absently with his long fingers as he studied the screen.

A sudden shiver ran up his spine as realization struck him like a wave from the cold pacific. "This might be it."

He swiveled his high-backed plush office chair and studied the dust-covered wall of travel books that lined the walls of his study. Stream of golden rays of sunlight cut through the dust bunnies that floated and danced in the stream of heaven like markers that poured in from the backyard. The window overlooked Charlotte's vegetable garden. The sweet, red tomatoes were due to be harvested later this afternoon when she returned from her appointment. But he knew he wouldn't be here to taste their burst of earthy flavor. No, he'd be on his way to Oregon.

He reached for the black portable com unit that always sat on his desk beside his computer interface. He punched the red on button and was met with silence. The battery was dead. He cursed softly. "When I'm focused I'm really focused. Damn," he muttered.

He hurried from the room and walked into the bright canary yellow kitchen to where the banana-shaped phone was attached to the wall. Charlotte had found this treasure so delightful at that charity auction last year. He hated the damn thing.

He picked the old fashioned receiver from its cradle and dialed the number of the airline he always used. A woman's voice answered after two rings.

"Welcome to Orbit Shuttle. Please note…" the automated message continued for several seconds until Trevor hit the back door code to bypass the automated menus.

Ever since the message service companies realized everyone knew to hit zero, or some other specific number to connect with a live person, they'd made it increasingly difficult to get through the menus. Trevor had befriended many of the shuttle company's employees in his travels and he was privy to the preferred customer code. Only the most frequent flyers were allowed this level of access. After over two thousand flights, in the past five years he'd become the most frequent flyer they'd ever had.

Ever since you'd been able to get from LA to Paris in two hours his hops and jumps around the world were becoming more the norm than the exception so he'd likely loose his preferred status soon enough.

One ring and someone picked up. "How may I help you?" said an over friendly male voice. He cringed inside but pressed on.

"Huh..Hi, this is Trevor Watkins. I'd like to book a shuttle flight to Lincoln City, Oregon please." He knew that when he said his name it would trigger the voice recognition software in the OSB System to bring his history file up on the screen sitting in front of the booking agent.

As usual it did. "Certainly, Mr. Watkins. And may I say sir this will be your two thousandth and thirteen flight with us so it will be charged at half the normal rate." Trevor allowed himself a smile. The OBS had been bribing him with half fares since flight one thousand and one, though he never got tired of the supposed discount. With security fees, state, federal and local taxes it didn't mean much anyway. But maybe with the savings Charlotte would be able to afford her pumpkin seeds for the fall pumpkin-growing contest she entered every year.

"Would you prefer coach or first class?"

"Coach as usual," Trevor said, knowing full well the agent could easily see that he'd flown coach on every flight he'd ever taken with the shuttle service.

The agent finished the booking then accepted his credit code for the purchase. Trevor felt a sense of relief. At least there was enough to pay for the trip in the account. "Thank the God's of travel," he muttered as he fled the room to begin packing.

A couple of day's worth of clothes and toiletries were all he'd need. And he'd leave a note for Charlotte. He was sure she'd understand. At least he hoped so.

\*\*\*

When he entered the small shuttle terminal in Lincoln City from the wind-swept tarmac, he ran his fingers through his shoulder length dark pepper sprinkled hair. The ocean breezes often played havoc with his hair. He brushed it away from his eyes with one hand all the while maintaining his iron grip with the other on his worn and faded leather briefcase. It was a family heirloom left to him by his father.

He headed for the baggage pickup in the small terminal A bored red cap stood leaning on his anti-grav luggage trolley waiting for someone to approach who needed help. In the front of the terminal was where the hover cars and sky buses waited to take arriving passengers to the string of seaside hotels and resorts that dotted this section of the Oregon coast. Gambling, beachcombing, and partying were the sports of interest to anyone who usually visited this part of the world. None of these pursuits held any interest for Trevor.

He stood by the baggage drop and tapped one cowboy booted foot to mark his impatience while his sunglasses that shielded eyes allowed him to study his fellow passengers. It was a hobby of his. A way to collect characters for the great American novel he planned to write someday.

A steel gray haired man, on the high side of sixty, dressed in an impeccable navy pin striped suit, white shirt and red power tie, stood patiently watching the numbers of the arriving shuttles as they flashed on the baggage drop screen. Their luggage would materialize shortly once it was put through the reconfigure device used by the major carriers these days. Gone were the days when luggage consumed so much take off weight. Their luggage was reduced in weight by molecular reconfiguration to lighter than air materials. Once they arrived at their destination, the luggage was reconfigured into its original form. Worked like a charm every time.

Trevor spotted a young couple who looked to be on their honeymoon snuggling and holding hands. They gazed longingly into each other's eyes. Trevor vividly recalled the times he and Charlotte had been like that. He recalled her perfume in his nostrils as he'd nuzzled her neck, and the softness of her lips as he kissed them.

He shook off the memories before they threatened to overwhelm him. His one regret was not being with Charlotte much over the last five years. It was hard on them both to be apart so much. If it weren't for the thrill of the chase, he'd have abandoned the project long ago.

Finally, the ground crew arrived with the glass tube that contained everyone's luggage. The two workers, one man the other a woman, gingerly placed the glass tube, that reminded Trevor of Mr. Billings beakers in his tenth grade biology class, on the platform. Within seconds, there was an eruption of light as a burst of energy was released. After the flash faded, and the spots before Trevor's eyes cleared, the luggage that belonged to shuttle flight thirteen passengers stood in three neat rows ready to go.

Trevor spotted his small, maroon colored hard sided over night case. Charlotte said it looked like a woman's makeup bag, an observation he didn't appreciate.

He picked up his bag then looked for the rental car company he'd booked before leaving home. It was the same one he'd used many times before.

After the crowd of passengers had somewhat dissipated, he finally saw the rental agency booth against the far wall near the exit doors.

There was no one behind the desk.

He walked over then bent down to place his bag and briefcase on the polished marble floor next to him. He straightened to find the clerk's smiling features watching him. Behind the counter was a young blond woman with one of those "how can I help you" smiles on her high cheek-boned face. Her blue eyes sparkled in the low light of the terminal. The perfect service industry employee, thought Trevor.

He smiled briefly in return then said, "I believe you have a reservation under the name, Watkins?"

"The woman's eyes traveled over her screen set below the counter, aligned so she was the only one who could see it. She nodded. "Yes, sir. Two days is it?"

"Yes, that's right."

She held out a small pad upon which he pressed the thumb of his right hand. This would verify his identity and debit his credit account for the charges. He waited while the system ran through its checks.

He felt a sense of unease as the woman's eyes flitted over the screen then up at him. Her smile widened as the checks came back positive.

There was an audible click. The rental system computer had created the starter card encoded with his information and access permission. The card and his thumbprint would be needed to start the car.

Without both pieces of information the vehicle disabler would come on, the doors would lock, and a signal would be sent to the police to investigate.

He thanked the young woman, (whose plastic nametag said she was Pam) then turned and left the terminal. The hover cars for rent were lined in a neat row near the one story building. He walked down the line of shiny new vehicles until he came to the number indicated on the starter card. It was one of the perks of traveling to drive the newer models. His car at home was a fifty-seven whose best years were far in the past.

The hover car selected for him was a canary yellow two-door coupe. Kinda sporty, he thought. Even so, it would be underpowered so no fancy racing about this trip.

He placed his over night bag in the trunk, but decided to keep his briefcase in the front seat with him on the passenger seat. He wasn't about to take any chances losing his baby.

He started the engine by inserting the card in the slot in the dashboard. It came to life purring as contentedly as a satisfied kitten. He felt the surge of power run through the little compact. He engaged the flight controls with a brief touch of the steering column and the car lifted gently off the ground.

151

The autopilot engaged and he eased back in the seat getting comfortable as the seat molded itself to conformed to his lanky writer's body

Soon he was clear of the shuttle port parking lot headed south on the 101. He idly studied the massive homes and resorts that lined the expressway as they crawled forward in the stream of traffic. The car would handle the traffic without his intervention, which was considerable on this stretch of highway at this time of year. It was spring and the snowbirds were heading south in droves.

He pressed the button for the satellite tracking system and the face of the dashboard rolled up to reveal a small screen. It came on and showed him where he was in relation to his destination. He'd already pre-entered his destination when he booked the car so the on-board computer would know the way.

He felt a surge of excitement as he noted that they were within thirty minutes of arrival. The traffic ahead was slow so the four kilometers would take an eternity. He pushed the negative thoughts away as he realized he might finally be coming to the end of his quest.

\*\*\*

He glided past the strip mall twice as the car went back and forth over the same stretch of highway. The autopilot bleated at him every time he passed the spot just before the bridge that separated Nelscott from Taft. He puzzled over this.

How could the computer be telling him he'd missed his destination when it didn't appear to exist at all? Finally, he'd had enough. There was a gift shop on the Nelscott side of the bridge. He took control of the hover controls and steered the car into the parking lot.

He got out and went inside. A teenage looking boy, probably no more than eighteen, stood behind the waist-high laminated counter of the Nelscott Gift Emporium and Book Shop as he walked in. Trevor preferred to ask directions in stores that sold books. It seemed to him that readers were a tight community and could more easily relate to other readers. And besides writers were like Gods to these people. Or so he'd experienced in the past when he'd explained he was a writer conducting research. They'd fall all over themselves to help him.

He strolled to the counter with a slight smile on his narrow features. The bespectacled teenager with short brown hair and watery hazel eyes glanced up when he heard the door open.

His expression was bland and he didn't show any sign of a reaction to Trevor's easy charm. Am I losing my touch? he thought.

"Hi, I'm lost. I was wondering if you could give me directions."

The teen shrugged his broad shoulders. Trevor could see the teenager was built like a football player, with an expansive chest and wide shoulders underneath his forest green sweatshirt that said Auburn across the front in gold lettering.

"Yeah, sure."

"Great. I'm looking for Almost. Do you know where it is?"

The teenage shrugged. "Nope. Sorry. Never heard of it. I'm just here for the summer. You'll have to talk to one of the locals."

Trevor nodded and gave the teen a brief smile. "Is there someone else here that might know?"

"Let me check."

The teenager left Trevor standing at the counter as he disappeared through an arch behind him guarded by a bead curtain where the storeroom must be.

Trevor stood his booted foot tapping out the latest Broadway musical he'd heard over the sound system on the shuttle until, after several moments, the young man reappeared followed by an older woman.

She wore old-fashioned granny glasses, and her straight gray hair was pulled into a ponytail. Her craggy features broke into a sparkling white smile when she saw him standing there. She wore khaki shorts, brown sandals and a smoke gray sleeveless shirt. A few beads of perspiration dotted her creased forehead.

She held out one weathered hand. "Trevor Watkins isn't it?" she said in a surprisingly youngish sounding voice.

"Huh…yes. Do I know you?" He took her hand in his. Her grip was firm and surprisingly warm. She looked just this side of eighty.

She shook her head. "Oh, no, but I know who you are from your picture on the jackets of your books. I never forget a face." She appeared thoughtful for a brief second. "I especially enjoyed the one about the antique New England rocking chairs. Fascinating, truly fascinating."

He released her hand and said, "I'm flattered indeed, madam. And impressed you even bothered to read that one."

She waved away his objections then a look of concern wrinkled her brow. "Oh my, I should have introduced myself. Elizabeth Salmon." She paused to place one arm around the waist of the young man, "And this young fella is my nephew, Peter."

The teenager smiled through pursed lips. He was obviously uncomfortable with his Aunts open display of affection.

"He's my sister's boy, on hiatus from college for the summer. I'm paying him a small salary to help him out, and keep him out of trouble." Peter blushed and turned away to disappear into the back room.

"So, Peter tells me you're looking for Almost." She placed her hands on her narrow hips and eyed him as if to gauge his reaction.

Trevor nodded. He liked this woman already and he'd only just met her. "Yes, do you know where I might find it?' She nodded then with one hand rubbed her chin. "Yes I do, Mr. Watkins….I just don't know if that's a place you really want to go."

"Why not? And please call me Trevor." The air was suddenly filled with mystery. Trevor felt the ache of excitement grow in his belly. He knew it! He'd been right. He didn't know how but this trip was different than all the others. He sensed the end of his travels were near, very near.

She nodded and the look in her eye told him she'd reached a decision. "Okay, Trevor. I'll take you," she said with a sly grin. She glanced behind her at the archway leading to the storeroom.

"Peter, you watch the store. I'll be back in a while."

"Okay, Auntie Betty." The echo of Peter's reply was followed by an audible grunt that marked physical labor. The boy was hard at work.

Betty smiled warmly then came around the counter that separated them to link one arm under Trevor's. "Where's your car?" she said in a musical lilt.

They walked to the parking lot then got into the rental hover car. Betty leaned over, then using the keypad attached to the internal guidance computer, as she keyed in the coordinates.

She smiled briefly and nodded as Trevor touched the flight controls as before and they lifted off. The engine purred softly in his ears and Betty's slight odor of jasmine now filled the car. He reveled in the smell of it. The scent reminded him of Charlotte's flower garden.

The car hovered at the entrance to the expressway as it waited for an opening in the traffic. Finally both lanes were clear and the car accelerated pressing them both back in the conform seats, the servomotors straining audibly to keep them as comfortable as possible. To Trevor's surprise, they had crossed the highway to the other side.

There was an ancient gravel turn off. A left over from the days when wheeled vehicles ruled the highways and byways.

The car floated across the wide expanse of gravel until he saw an opening in the forest greenery that was invisible from the main road. To his surprise it was a road, of sorts. Not much of one, really. To be honest it looked more like an ancient wagon path than a road. Branches from low hanging trees crowded the narrow road as the car proceeded down the well-traveled path. Arm like branches of pines and oaks scrapped over the polished surface of the car. Trevor cringed each time heavy coarse needles ran down the roof and sides of the expensive car. He was certain he'd lose his insurance deductible.

Betty seeing his discomfort chuckled lightly. "Don't worry, Trevor. You'll never see a mark." Somehow, he doubted her.

Finally, after ten minutes they were approaching a clearing. An ancient wooden single story building with peeling paint, and a single door with a screen door that hung limply off its hinges came into view. Upon seeing it, Trevor began to doubt the old woman. Maybe she had screw loose.

"Here we are," she said brightly, as the hover car came to a halt next to the dilapidated structure then dropped gently to the grass covered meadow that surrounded the time–worn building.

"Where is here?" Trevor said as he studied the sad looking structure intently. It looked as if it were a hundred years old at least or maybe older. It's a wonder it hadn't collapsed long ago. The wood was gray and weathered and the little chips of sky blue paint that were left were likely the only thing holding it together.

"Trevor Watkins, may I present Le Petite Café!" She burst into a wide smile as she flung the passenger door open and stepped out onto the wind bent grass. He watched her pause to fill her lungs with a deep breath of air.

For several seconds Trevor considered closing the doors and fleeing but he actually liked this old woman so he decided he better join in her fantasy.

He opened his door and was hit with the smells of the forest. The grass and trees ejected such a base cornucopia of nature at him that he felt suddenly at one with his surroundings. It was like those times when he was a kid and his father had taken him hiking in the hills surrounding their home in Lake Wenatchee.

He followed her as she headed for the broken down shack.

Reluctantly he walked after her shaking his head in sadness. She was a mad old woman. He should have known better after seeing the reactions of her nephew. If the young man were really her nephew and if his name was actually Peter, which he doubted.

At the door, she waited for him, then as he approached, she opened it with flourish and stepped inside. It looked dark inside.

He squinted then stepped through. He blinked once then found himself standing inside a brightly lit room that looked like those old-fashioned roadside diners he'd seen in period movies.

A man with a slate gray goatee, wearing a black western hat with a colorful band of gold and silver round the center was busy wiping the shiny apple red lunch counter with a white cloth as they came in. The smell of coffee and fresh baked apple pie permeated the room. There was a row of polished steel stools with ruby-colored cushions atop them, as if they were cherry Popsicles. The row of empty stools was broken by a lone figure that sat on the one farthest from the door.

The man wiping the counter glanced up from his work as they entered and smiled warmly. "Hey, Betty long time no see."

"Hey yourself Hardee," Betty said nodding toward Trevor, "Brought a guest with me."

"Yeah I can see that. We've been expecting him."

Trevor's eyes went wide as Betty guided him to the counter where they each took a seat beside each other.

"So where you been?" said Hardee gazing at Betty.

"My sister's boy is with me this summer and I have to keep on eye on him. You know what these teenagers can be like."

Hardee's indigo eyes sparkled and he laughed lightly. "Yeah, I know what you mean."

"What did you mean?" blurted Trevor when he'd regained sufficient composure.

The figure at the end of counter spoke up interrupting Hardee before he could reply. "He means how did you know he was comin'?"

Trevor glanced toward this new voice, a man's voice. At the end of the lunch counter sat a man, who from the look of him had to be seven feet in height, if he was an inch. His voice contained an odd echoing quality to it as if he were speaking from the bottom of a well. His sleeveless arms were covered in tattoos that ran from his bare shoulders to his wrists.

He was tanned like someone who'd worked outdoors all his life. Dark jet-black curls stuck out from beneath the brim of an Australian bush hunter's hat two sizes too small for his huge head. His dark eyes seemed to bore into Trevor sending a shiver of dread through him.

"Oh knock off the drama will ya, Milt," said Hardee with a laugh. "Don't worry about him." Hardee waived his hand at Milt who went back to sipping from a white china coffee cup. The giants wide grin made Trevor feel even more ill at ease.

The door that Trevor assumed led to the kitchen suddenly was thrown open and a large purple slug with wings floated through. A white paper chef's hat sat perched atop what must be the head, as it was the end facing forward as it flew. Web-like wings stuck out from its body two feet to either side. Trevor raised one trembling index finger at the being unable to utter a single sound. His jaw hung open as he stared at the slug thing. He was frozen to his seat.

Hardee rolled his eyes. "Wally, didn't I tell you to stay in the back until I told the lad a little more about us?"

The slug thing, somehow dubbed Wally, shrugged and lifted on the air stirred by its wings floated to the row of soda dispensers against the roughed pine wall. An arm appeared from its purple gelatin like body. It seemed to grow from its body before his eyes. It used this newly created arm to grasp a drink glass it retrieved from under the counter. Another arm appeared and it drew itself a glass of cola. "Sorry, H. I was getting' thirsty. It's friggin' hot back there ya know." Its voice was normal, sort of sounded human with a slight Texas drawl.

Wally must be from Texas, thought Trevor.

The purple slug paused to hover in front of him. Trevor felt the air from the action of its wings waft over him. All he could smell was the odor of the cola.

"Sorry. Hope you're havin' a nice day," said Wally. The sincerity in its voice was unmistakable.

"Huh…sure no problem…"

Wally the flying purple slug left them alone once again when he disappeared through the door he'd come in by.

"Where the hell am I," said Trevor gazing at Hardee then turning his attention to Betty who shrugged, a small knowing smile on her lips.

"Now, Trevor my boy…" began Hardee.

Trevor gave the diner owner a warning look then focused his attention on the old woman. Her smile disappeared and her eyes dropped to the counter. After a momentary pause she gazed hard into his eyes. Hers were now were tinged with pain.

"Trevor, I know this will be very hard to understand, but your mother wasn't of this world. She was from outside. Another place. Another dimension." She paused and pointed at the door where Wally had disappeared only seconds before. "That's where Wally and all of us here came from. That's the place Elizabeth came from." She waved one hand around then continued. "This place, this diner is our refuge. A place where we come to get away from the world you've always known as home. A place where, as the kids are so find of saying, 'We can let our hair down'." She gazed at him her eyes watery.

"Do you understand?"

Trevor shook his head. "No, not really…" But from somewhere deep inside he realized he did know what they were talking about. He'd been drawn here. This was home.

Hardee smiled "We know why you're here, Trevor my boy. You're here to find the perfect cup of coffee, of course."

Trevor looked at the coffee shop man through narrowed eyes. How did he know that? He'd not said anything to Betty or anyone else about why he was coming here. He'd not even taken the time to leave that note for Charlotte. No one knew why he was here. No one except his loyal followers…yes, that had to be it.

"You've been to my website?"

"Sorry, old fella we don't have one of those 'puters round here." As if to emphasize his point Hardee's eyes moved around the room. Betty snickered behind her hand, her gray eyes dancing with amusement.

Now Trevor was really bewildered. "Well, then how did you know I was coming?"

Hardee smiled warmly, moved to the wall behind him, and retrieved a white china cup like the one Milt was sipping from, and a matching saucer. He hadn't noticed it there before but Trevor realized he was looking at the largest collection of glass tubing this side of the bio-lab at MIT. The tubing ran in loops and curves like a fragile nest of clear wires. At one end sat an oval shaped bowl that contained boiling water. Then bubbling water traveled through the glass tubes until it ended at a pile of dark Earthen looking powder.

From here it was pushed upward (by what means he had no idea, as it seemed to defy gravity) until it connected to a tube filled with the now darkened liquid ending at a spout with a tap. Hardee eyes smirked at Trevor as he moved to moved to spout. He opened the tap after placing the cup and saucer underneath and there was the sound of running water until the cup was filled to the brim. Hardee then came back to place the cup in front of Trevor with a click of china on arborite.

"This is how. And why."

Trevor hesitated with his confused gaze fixed on the black steaming liquid that filled the cup to the brim. There was a steel creamer in front of him and a bowl of snow-white sugar next to it. He picked up a metal spoon and placed one heaping spoon of sugar in the cup then a dollop of cream form the creamer. He was certain he'd regret this, but he took the cup in both hands and brought it to his lips.

The heavenly aroma that assaulted him quickly overwhelmed his senses. A flood of memories filled his mind as the mixture of odors permeated his every bodily orifice. He pictured his sweet mother on that day all those years ago. Her toothpaste smile, her hazel eyes, her healthful flushed cheeks.... He stopped the cup in mid-air and felt a rush of grief wash over him.

He replaced the cup on the saucer as tears welled in his eyes. "Why?" he managed to croak before his voice choked in his throat.

"It's alright, Trevor," said Betty softly taking his hand in hers.

Trevor turned to look at her, tears blinding her features to him as the salty trails of moisture began run in rivulets down his cheeks.

"There, there," she cooed. He moved toward her and buried his face in her shoulder. She cupped his head gently and murmured words of encouragement.

Finally, the feeling passed and Trevor managed to sit up. He again the raised the cup to his lips and this time successfully swallowed some. It tasted ordinary. Bitter. Not at all what he'd expected. He replaced the cup once more.

"She was one of us," said Hardee.

"One of what?" said Trevor.

"I think you know," said Betty taking both of his hands in hers and gazing deep into his eyes. He nodded. Of course, he knew. He'd always known.

***

Trevor sat perched on the edge of his chair pounding furiously at his keyboard when he heard Charlotte walk in.

167

The words seemed to flow from his fingers to the screen as if he were taking dictation.

He swiveled his office chair to face his wife a wide grin pasted to his face as she entered. She reeked of perm solution, which would normally bother him, but instead it was the most pleasant smell on the planet.

"How's the book coming?" she said.

"Almost finished."

She chuckled. "Wonderful. What do you want to do to celebrate?"

"How about a holiday?"

"What a great idea! Where do you want to go?"

"How about the Oregon coast?"

"Why there?"

Trevor shrugged. "Oh, I don't know. Maybe it's because Mom loved the place. And they do have the best coffee in the universe."

"Okay." Charlotte shrugged then turned and left the room closing the door behind her.

He smiled to himself. Yeah, the coffee may be instant but the place was magic.

# Lock, Stock, and Barrel

SIMON GRUNTED AS HE DROPPED to his knees on the dusty shop floor. His knees cracked and a sharp pain pinched his lower back. Simon Pyman felt older than dirt.

He squinted at the damaged heel in the poor light.

Lying on his stomach he thumbed the button on the flashlight in his left hand and a cone of white light illuminated the back of Shapiro's foot. He knew he should buy stronger light bulbs, but since he's a cheap man he didn't.

The simulacrum stood like a statue as Simon peered closely at the tear in the plasti-skin. It seemed sim's were always breaking down. His hazel eyes narrowed. "There it is," he muttered.

Using his index finger Simon pulled out the damaged wire from the tear in the sim's plasti-skin.

Shapiro must've caught his foot on something to tear a hole this big. It wasn't surprising to him Shapiro was having trouble given the size of the tear. Wires don't take kindly to Windmill's rainy, cold weather.

He eyed the hole and saw rainwater had collected inside the tear at the bottom of the heel like a cup.

"Wally?" he said glancing over this shoulder at his assistant Wally Ogdon seated on a molded plastic chair near the workbench across the cluttered workshop. In his greasy hands Wally held a sandwich comprised of two slices of white bread, mayonnaise, and cloned cheese. Wally ate the same thing every day since he started as assistant mechanic. He wasn't much of a mechanic, but Simon couldn't be too choosey given there were very few humans' left of the original colonists. Not that Wally himself was an original. He came later.

Wally looked up from studying his meal, his sea green eyes questioning. "Yeah, boss?"

Simon chuckled. "How many times do I have to tell you not to call me boss? My name's Simon." As if telling him for the millionth time is going to change anything. Wally's eyes drooped.

"Never mind," he said cringing. Wally was too sensitive for his own good.

"Sorry. Bring me the soldering gun will you? Shapiro needs a tune up."

"Looks like he stepped in a rabbit hole to me," said Wally with a shrug. He stood, placed his sandwich on a plain brown wrapper on the workbench, and then went to retrieve the soldering gun from the cubbyhole above the bench where Simon kept it.

Wally walked toward him cradling the tool in his pale hands as if it were a baby. He's going to make a good nurse someday.

After handing Simon the soldering gun Wally dropped to his haunches and peered at the damage to the sim's foot.

"There're no rabbits on Windmill," said Simon. His eyes crinkled at the corners. "But you know that."

Wally's mouth formed a thin smile and he blew at a lock of carrot-colored hair that had fallen across his face. "Kilroy rats are kinda like rabbits."

Simon shifted his gaze back to the task at hand and brought the tip of the soldering gun closer to the wire. "Rabbits with razor sharp teeth aren't rabbits."

Pressing the trigger on the gun caused the tip to become white hot, while at the same producing a stream of liquid metal that coated the wire. "There," he said with satisfaction. "One more thing and we're done."

He handed the soldering gun to Wally who carried it to the bench and returned with a small plastic packet containing white powder. He handed it to Simon.

A bell sounded coming from the direction of the reception counter at the front of the shop. Simon closed his eyes and sighed. What now? I'm just about done.

"Go see who it is," he said to Wally.

"Okay, boss." He heard Wally's shuffling footsteps as he left to see who was at reception.

After his assistant was gone he opened his eyes and studied the tear in the plasti-skin. About three ounces should do it.

He pulled the zip lock across the top of the packet then poured a small pile of the powder on the shop floor. The smell of vanilla emanating from the powder filled his nostrils. That looks about right.

"Hey, boss," said Wally startling him. He sneezed and the powder blew away.

"Wally!"

"Oops. Sorry, boss."

Simon's next words were going to be you're fired, but he knew he couldn't fire him he liked Wally too much.

"A guy out front really wants to talk to you."

"A guy? And?" Simon got off the floor using his hands to brush shop dust and the remnants of the plasti-skin repair compound off his coveralls.

"And he's a real estate guy."

A knot formed in Simon's belly. Someone had finally answered the ad.

"Ok." Simon paused. He had to remain cool. He didn't want to look as anxious as a virgin bride on her wedding night. "Good."

He buried his trembling hands in the long pockets of his coveralls. "What's he look like?"

"I don't know." Wally's pale forehead wrinkled. "A guy. Tall, thin, wearing a fancy suit, and his shoes look expensive. Antrim lizard skin I'd say."

He stared at his assistant. "Whoa, have you been watching the fashion vids again?"

Wally smirked. "I wasn't always a mechanic's assistant."

Slapping Wally on his shoulder Simon laughed. "Of course not. How's about we catch Suz's show at the Ol' Miner one day after work and you tell me all about it."

"Sure," he shrugged. "Why not?"

"Why don't you finish fixing ol' Shapiro here and I'll go talk to the real estate guy. Sound good?"

"Sure."

When Simon entered the lobby the man Wally described was seated in the cloned leather chair next to the glass door. What Wally neglected to tell him the guy wasn't human, even if he wore human clothes. The blue skin of the back of his hands looked rough to the touch. He's a Thom.

Thom's reputation as the ultimate salesmen in the galaxy is well known, even on the outer rim worlds like Windmill. And Windmill is the farthest planet from the galactic core.

Alien or human he was just grateful someone finally responded to his ad.

Thom's don't shake hands so Simon was grateful he could keep his hands buried in his pockets. "Hi. Can I help you?"

The Thom stood up and Simon realized Wally wasn't exaggerating. He was a bigun all right, must be at least a seven footer.

"Mr. Pyman?" Simon smiled and nodded. "My name's Cinder Burns." He reached into the inside pocket of his grey suit jacket and pulled out a business card which he offered to Simon.

Simon pulled his right hand out of the pocket of his coveralls, pleased to see it had stopped shaking, and accepts the card.

His bladder screamed when he read Cinder Burns name over the title Uniserve Collection Agency. That's one of Andre Champions shell companies. He quickly stuffed his hand back in his pocket when it began to tremble.

"What can I do for you?"

The Thom smiled making Simon slightly queasy. When a Thom smiles its lips roll back to reveal its purple gums and double rows of yellow teeth. Burns said, "I represent an interested buyer."

Suppressing his revulsion Simon pocketed Burns's card and then crossed his arms over his chest and leaned his lean frame against the wall. He frowned. "What does this buyer want to pay for the planet?"

The Thom blew air from its single nasal hole in the middle of its face between the mouth and the black eyes. "The buyer wishes to buy you."

"Me?" Simon straightened. "I thought this is about my ad."

"Ad?"

"Yes. I'm selling the planet lock, stock and barrel."

"The planet?" Burns emitted a mixture of growl, groan and guffaw throwing his large hairless head back in the process.

He had never heard a Thom laugh before. At least he hoped it was laughter. It sounded more like a cow in heat.

"No, Mr. Pyman. I'm sorry but the buyer's not interested in the planet. After the failure of the colony and the terra forming project twenty six years ago no one is interested in this property." Burns approached the counter. Simon's nose wrinkled and resisted the urge to take a step back and pinch his nose. A Thom's breath reeks of sour milk.

"We have minerals," said Simon matter-of-factly. "The sims discovered a vein of lime quartz just the other day."

The Thom laughed again turned and headed for the front door. Through the glass door Simon saw the glittering rain that fell in sheets from the billowing clouds that crowded the sky day and night.

Rain. It always rains. What was he thinking? Only a duck would buy this planet.

He glanced at the digital clock on the wall to the left of the door. It was almost closing time.

"Think about it, Mr. Pyman." Burns pushed against the aluminum bar across the door but stopped after it opened part way and swiveled his head to gaze at Simon.

"Simon Pyman?" he shook his head in a very human manner. "Really? A nursery rhyme? Bit simple don't you think?"

After Burns disappeared into the gathering gloom Simon took a deep breathe. He's a bounty hunter. They knew where he was. Now what is he going to do?

***

After he sent Wally home for the day he hurried to his apartment over Rosie's Bar and Grill. He even hired an air taxi, unusual given the cost and his modest income from the shop.

Seated behind the plasti-steel desk his fingertips brushed the hidden button under the desktop. He rolled his chair back pushing with his feet as the desktop swung upward to reveal a thin, flat screen. Within milliseconds the screen lit up to reveal a smiling blonde woman.

"Yes, darling?" said the image. Today she wore his favorite ruby red spaghetti strap cocktail dress. His mouth formed a wry smile. He'd grown to love this new interface with his AI. Wally was a genius with AI's.

He pulled his chair forward with his feet until his stomach bumped against the edge of the desk.

The blue-eyed blonde gazed at him with a loving expression on her angular features.

"Hey, Jill. I need transportation. Fast."

"I will summon a taxi, sweetie. Fast." Jill's tone was edged with disappointment.

"No, Jill!" He knew his nerves were really on edge. Stupid. "Sorry, Jill. I didn't mean local transportation. I mean off planet. I mean out of system. I mean anywhere in the galaxy BUT here, and as soon as possible, preferably sooner."

"Is there a problem, lovey?" Jill purred and her perfect digital mouth formed a sensual pout.

"Of course not, Jill my love I just received an e-gram from my aunt saying my favorite uncle left me a Monastery on Zebra II and I want to collect is all."

"I don't recall any e-gram, darling." Now she sounded like a little girl.

"No. Wally went to check the public boards for me and brought it to me."

"But, huny bun —"

"Never mind, Jill, it doesn't matter," Simon cut her off. "Have you found me transportation?" AI's were capable of processing forty-seven billion terabytes of data simultaneously. Jill could solve the riddles of the universe, seduce him, check his mail, and hopefully find him a way off Windmill all within milliseconds.

"Yes. The Marketeer FTL ship Moby Dick currently in orbit is scheduled to depart at 0640 tomorrow morning. It has three passenger spaces available for purchase." Jill paused. Simon frowned. She must think he was going to yell at her again.

"Do you wish me to book passage, Simon?"

Burns must expect to have him in custody by the time that ship leaves. And dead or alive probably wasn't a condition of his contract. "No. Thank you, Jill, but no."

He eased back in the chair and thought for a second. One eyebrow arched on his forehead. He was afraid to ask. "Is there anything else? Any other ship?"

"According to the galactic ship masters records there are no vessels scheduled to arrive at Windmill for the next two solar years."

Simon slumped in his chair. That was it, he was sunk. Burns will take him back to Telex Two and Andre Champions goons will tear him up.

He stood and walked to the window over looking the street. The rain had stopped and the clouds had parted after months of steady rain. The twin moons appeared in the western sky to cast a soft white glow over the street scene below.

Various Sims walked past carrying purchases for their owners while some worker sims, still in their rain coats, used shovels to dig mud out of the gutters by the side of the road.

He should never have let Max convince him to steal from Champion. Gangsters don't like it when you rob them. Even if it's the perfect crime. He sighed and watched Shapiro come into view. The simulacrum had a small teacup sized dog tethered on a leash. The dog's eyes were hidden by long fur that covered its tiny body and dragged on the ground. The hair waved like a curtain of hair in time to its bouncy step.

That gives me an idea.

Walking back to the desk he sat down and gazed into Jill's patient azure pools. "Jill, who can create a simulacrum?"

She hesitated. "Be more specific, please."

"Sorry." He rolled his eyes. He was saying sorry a lot lately. "I mean a sim of an actual human."

The perfectly smooth skin of Jill's brow furrowed slightly. "That procedure is illegal, Simon. The Galactic Senate outlawed human copying in 4213."

Since when is she a lawyer? "Yes, I know, Jill but if I wanted a simulacrum of me for say a week or so where would I get it?"

Without hesitation Jill said, "There is one black market dealer currently on Windmill." There was a hint of disapproval in her tone. But who cares what an AI thinks?

"Show me the address." His eyes widened when it appeared on the screen.

That's my shop.

\*\*\*

Wally's apartment on Monitor Street is on the top floor of a four-story brick walkup. The outside looked like one of those ancient brick buildings he'd seen in history books, only these bricks were constructed from a carbon/titanium/steel/diamond alloy harder than steel. Wally's building dated back eighty years to the first colonist's arrival on Windmill.

He's going to give me some answers, and he's going to build him a sim before morning. Simon looked both ways on the dark street. No sign of Burns. His stomach muscles tightened. It felt like a net was closing in around him.

Pulling back the sleeve of his raincoat he looked at the watch on his wrist. 0043. Time is definitely running out.

His heart pounded in his chest as he raced up the stairs until he finally stood outside apartment 402. There were only two apartments on the top floor.

Wally could never afford this apartment on the salary he paid him. He assumed he made extra money upgrading AI's. He never would have thought his assistant traded in black market tech.

Still breathing hard he pressed his hand on the touch panel recessed into the wall next to the doorframe. After several seconds of waiting a simulacrum opened the door. Tall, with oil black hair the male sim looked at Simon as if he were an insect. "We do not accept deliveries outside business hours," he said in a clipped tone.

"Never mind that crap," Simon gasped his hand resting against the door frame, "I need to see Wally Ogdon," he paused to take in a deep breath, "right now."

"I'm sorry but the Master is not receiving visitors at this hour. Please come back later." Simon stuck his foot between the door and the frame.

Simon winced when the sim closed the door on his foot. "Listen, I'm Wally's boss. If he doesn't see me immediately you tell him he's fired. Got it?"

The sim eyed him through the gap between the door and the frame and arched an eyebrow.

"One moment, sir." It walked away leaving the door open.

Simon peered through the partially open door and saw very expensive furniture inside. The black market sim business must be good. His eyes locked on what could only be a real leather couch. He whistled softy. Correction. Very, <u>very</u> good.

He almost fell when the door suddenly swung open. Wally ran his pale fingers through his unruly orange hair yawning. "Sorry, boss. Jackson's manners are terrible. Com'on in." He stepped back and Simon walked into the apartment.

"Have a seat on the couch," he waved in the direction of the leather couch. "Ya wanta beer?"

"Huh, no. Thanks." Simon smiled thinly. He moved to the couch and sank into the soft cushion.

Wally shrugged, waved the sim away, and then shuffled to the matching leather chair opposite the couch his slippers shushing across the thick rug. The sim disappeared into a hallway leading off the living room.

Simon cleared his throat. "Wally, why have you been using the shop for your black market business?"

"Why have you been using the name Simon Pyman?"

Simon felt his cheeks grow warm. "Why not? It's my name."

Wally chuckled and eased back in the chair his arms flat on the chair arms. "No, it's not. Mr. Abram Shakespeare, former resident of Telex Two, and former hired gun for one Mr. Andre Champion."

How does he know? Simon's face paled and his hands began to tremble. Wally might be another bounty hunter.

As if reading his mind Wally added, "Don't worry I'm not a bounty hunter." He stood and walked to the fridge. He opened the door and pulled two brown beer bottles from the slot in the door. He popped the tops with his thumbs. "I'm a mechanic just like you." He walked over and handed Simon one of the beers. "Among other things."

"I don't know what you're talking about." When in doubt deny.

Wally shook his head then walked to the window. His eyes narrowed as he looked out then tipped back the bottle and took a long swig.

The bottle felt cold in Simon's hand. "Alright, Wally let's assume you know who I am. Where do we go from here?" His chances of him building him a sim had evaporated.

Wally shrugged. "What ya got to trade?"

"Trade? For what?"

Wally turned away from the window and shuffled back across the thick carpet. The chair sighed as he sat down. His green eyes were hard as stone, his lips a thin line. The beer bottle was pressed between his hands.

"A one way ticket to a planet so far away Champions people will never find you."

Simon felt beads of sweat tickle his back. "How far is that exactly?" If they found me on Windmill there is no place in the galaxy far enough to hide from Andre Champion.

Wally smirked then raised the bottle to his lips and took a sip. "Too far."

Simon sat forward on the couch until he was on the edge of the cushion. "What do I have to do?"

A slow smile formed on Wally's features. "Trade me Windmill."

Windmill? Is he kidding? Simon had been trying to dump this worthless hunk of rock ever since he won it a poker game fifteen years ago.

A sound of an air taxi's engine from the direction of the street outside made Simon tense. "Ok," he said fighting the desperation in his voice. "When can I leave?"

"Right now." Wally stood and walked to a door that until now Simon thought was a closet. He opened it.

Shielding his eyes with his hands from the sudden bright light Simon shot to his feet. "Is that what I think it is?"

"Yup. I traded a simulacrum for it with a guy who came through Windmill a year ago."

"Does it work?" Simon blinked away the tears and stared at the blue sky, green grass, and rolling hills on the other side of the open doorway.

Hard to believe, but it was a working dimensional portal. He'd never seen one outside books. Most people thought they were a myth. Now right before him was evidence they were real.

"Sure. I wouldn't be offering it if it didn't." Wally strode to the window and looked out. "Oh, oh, Mr. Burns brought a couple of Champions goons with him." He shook his head. "I don't think we gotta lot of time." His gaze shifted to Simon. "What do you say, we gotta a deal?"

Simon's eyes narrowed. He smelled a rat. "Where is that?" He nodded to the image on the other side portal.

"Somewhere in the Andromeda galaxy. Or so I'm told."

"So you're told?" It could be a ride to anywhere. That thing could be a simulation interface to fool him. The perfect escape, right into a trap.

Wally frowned and walked away from the window scratching his bare chest with his nails. "Listen, if you don't want the deal fine by me." He looked at Simon and smiled. "Nice knowing you, boss."

A sharp knock on the door made Simon tense. He had no choice. He had to get off planet now. "The deed to Windmill is in the floor safe under the work bench."

Wally nodded and took another swig from the beer bottle. "Yeah, I know where the safe is, but what's the combination?"

He found the safe? Never in his life had Simon pegged anyone so wrongly as Wally Ogdon. He really had him by the short hairs.

"Jill tells me everything," he added.

It dawned ion Simon, Wally added a back door into Jill's program. He knew everything him, everything he'd said to Jill on those lonely nights. The air was suddenly warmer.

"But I told Jill everything." Wally grinned and wiggled his eyebrows suggestively.

Time to give up. "The safe's voice activated. The combination is," he paused and his eyes flitted to the scene through the dimensional portal, "you sure about that?"

Wally nodded.

"The combination is alpha-three-seven-alpha."

Wally grunted as he stood, as did Simon. "Thanks, boss," he said. The pounding on the door intensified. "I don't think you have any time left."

"Yes." Simon paused and regarded his very clever, very scheming former assistant. "It's been a slice. Take care and thanks again."

Simon's last thought as he stepped through the door way to ask himself why Wally didn't use the portal himself then he was gone.

***

After opening the front door Wally sauntered back to the couch and plunked himself down. Cinder Burns came in, his black orbs focused on the open closet door. The scene through the portal had changed to a rocky beach, crashing surf, and wind bent palm trees.

"Is he gone?" said Burns.

"Yup." Wally tipped back his beer and drained the bottle.

After dropping the empty bottle on the couch next to him he emitted a loud burp.

Burns stood before the portal his fists balled on his hips studying the image. "Where did he go?"

Wally shrugged. "How would I know? I wouldn't use the thing. I don't know where anyone goes after they step through."

Burns turned to face him. "Did you get the deed?"

"Sure. I'll have it within the hour. Okay?" Wally avoided looking at the Thom knowing he'd be smiling.

"OK, Mr. Ogdon. That'll be fine." Burns strode to the window and looked out. "The weather here is perfect for us you know."

Wally nodded. "Yeah, I know." He frowned. "Does this settle my debt?"

"Oh, yes more than enough. As you humans are fond of saying; lock, stock, and barrel."

Wally glanced at the Thom standing peering out the window. "I'm leaving in the morning."

The Thom looked at him and nodded. "As I expected." Burns paused then added, "What do you imagine he's doing right now?"

Wally rose off the couch and started walking to the bedroom to dress and begin packing. "Having a beer with Andre I guess," he called before he disappeared down the hallway.

# Strange Bedfellows

I HATE THIS PLACE.

No, I wasn't trying to swim away from the island we'd been stranded on for the past six weeks. I just wanted a few minutes alone. Besides if I tried to swim away I'd either be cut to pieces on the sharp coral off shore or be eaten by sharks. Never mind the very real possibility of drowning.

With my head bobbing in the rolling blue-green surf surrounding me, I gazed at the sand of the beach that stretched out before me like a golden line in the ocean. The palm trees and ragged under brush beyond the beach seemed to stick out of the ocean itself.

Valentine and Alice sat with their hands flat in the sand behind them watching me from the beach on the small island where we were shipwrecked six weeks ago. The flesh of their exposed faces, arms, and hands were now glowed red form the blistering tropical sun.

The roar of the wild pacific striking the razor sharp coral five hundred yards behind me made communication with my wife, or our new friend, impossible. At any moment a moray eel, great white shark, or some similar monster of the deep, would swallow me whole and they would be unable to help me. Not that I was particularly worried. We'd not been fortunate enough to see such creatures in the lagoon in the time we'd been stranded here.

I'm not a strong swimmer, so my arms and legs were beginning to ache from the exertion, and my skin was beginning to wrinkle like some orange that has been in the sun too long. Too much desk time in my old life, I mused.

With my belly hanging over my faded gray shorts, and salt water invading my mouth, ears, and eyes, I began my methodical stroke, stroke, stroke toward the shore.

Not that I wanted to go back, I just had very little choice

Finally I was able to stand in the lapping waves. I dropped my feet to the wet sand as schools of tiny red, green, and blue fish tickled at my ankles and my feet. My legs felt heavy beneath me as I wadded ashore.

Once I was out of the water the hot sand burned the soles of my feet as I made my way, complaining with every step, toward the spot where the two women watched me, their eyes bored, their expressions listless.

Alice offered me a weak smile when I sat down beside her with a grunt. My wide butt caused a mini-shower of sticky sand that doused her hair and clothes. Lately our relationship had been rockier than smooth sailing. As our chance of rescue diminished so it seemed did our marriage.

"Oh, com'on," she growled as she tried without success to brush the grains of sand off her ample calves.

"Sorry," I said with a shrug. What was I going to say? It's not like I invented sand.

Alice grunted not looking at me. She must have sensed my apology wasn't exactly sincere, which it wasn't.

"Nice swim?" she asked equally insincerely.

"No." I shifted my butt and felt pinching grains of sand work their way into my groin area. It was impossible to get rid of the stuff entirely. "I can't get this sand outta my nooks and crannies no matter what I do," I said.

"Stop complaining, Rob," said Val chastised me. "You're giving me a headache."

Valentine (who preferred to be called Val) had been on the sailboat with us when it went down. The skipper had disappeared in the storm.

I caught Alice's eye with a glance. She arched an eyebrow at me and shrugged her wide shoulders. Her once smooth skin was becoming rough from the weeks of being stranded on this island. It was as if we were under assault by an army of sun, wind, and salt fairies. Very soon we'd all be one big piece of red leather.

I was really beginning to hate these two as much as the island. The tension between us had grown with each passing day rescue failed to arrive.

I gave my head a shake. I was loosing it for sure.

Our new friend, Valentine Motts, was a woman of substance in the real world, as she called it. "I'm a player," she explained on day one on this speck of sand in the south pacific. She said she was also low on her meds. What kind of meds she needed and what a player was exactly she never bothered to explain and I never bothered to ask.

I suspected her lack of medication was the reason for her increasingly irritability.

"Let's go back to camp," I said, "I think we've had enough surf and sand for one afternoon don't you think?"

Val snorted her disgust then stood and began to brush the clinging sand off her cutoffs and the arms of her white sleeveless blouse. Her long legs, indigo eyes, and heavy bosom attracted me to her the moment I laid eyes on her. The first time was six weeks ago when we woke up on the sand after the storm pounded the sailboat into the reef. The waves chopped the boat into kindling. In the dark we abandoned ship and swam for our lives. I still don't know how we survived the swim in the dark, but I do recall waking up to see Val, her wet clothes clinging to her voluptuous figure, lying on her side in front of me.

Out of the corner of my eye I caught Alice looking at me. Her smooth pinkish forehead was creased and her dark eyes burned a hole in me.

"What's the matter?" I said feigning ignorance.

Val had already headed for our makeshift camp above the tide line. Her footsteps muffled by the sand quickly retreated into the distance.

"You know what." Alice glared at me then stomped off her arms folded across her sagging breasts hidden beneath the green floral blouse she'd saved from the wreck.

She's more a stuff person than I am. Her feet were half buried in the soft sand as she walked away to leave me alone. My heart ached as I watched her go. How could she think this about me? Not that I hadn't given the idea of banging Val some thought these past few weeks, but it was stupid to think I'd actually do it. Alice knew I loved her. Didn't she?

I ran after my wife slipping on the sand like some drunken sailor on a weekend pass. I managed to mentally block out the searing heat of the sand as I ran.

I came up beside her. "Listen. Alice," I said breathing hard from the excretion. "It's not what you think —"

"Does it matter?"

"It does to me," I protested.

She stopped as we reached the brown earth bordering the beach. Her arms were still crossed across her smallish bosom and her eyes were filled with fire. "So?"

"What? I didn't do anything."

"You will." With that she walked off.

I watched her go knowing she was right. Or at least I wanted to, if Val wanted to. I can't imagine why she would want to sleep with a fat old fart like me, but desperate times make strange bedfellows.

***

Sitting with our backs to the ocean we watched in silence the crackling yellow and gold flames that leapt into the starlit sky. Our nightly fire consisted of palm tree logs that filled the air with dense pungent smoke.

I sat huddled between the two women on a log big enough to hold the three of us we'd dragged from the nearby forest of tall palm trees to act as our surrogate couch. We were seated upwind from the sooty, thick smoke of the fire carried in-land by the swirling winds coming off the ocean.

"One more day," said Val. Her tone was melancholy, filled with regret. I knew different. She didn't have choices any more than I did.

"Maybe we should split up?" suggested Alice. She used a stick she'd picked up from the chalky soil to poke at a burning log. This caused sparks to fly as if they were fireflies in some mad dance. The wood crackled loudly with each thrust of the stick.

"It won't do any good," said Val. Her gaze washed over me and I saw her eyes briefly flair then return to looking at a lump of burnt wood next to the fire. She wanted me. I knew it. Or was I imagining it? The hot sun and the thirst had made me doubt my sanity.

What was I going to do? My stomach began to complain and a vague taste of bile entered my mouth.

I moved to the lean-to we used to store the supply of coconuts and fruit we'd managed to collect from the trees and bushes farther in-land. I took half of one coconut and a piece of fruit that looked and tasted like a mango. I don't know if that's what it was, but it tasted okay, and it hadn't made me ill. Unlike some of the other fruit on this island I'd tried.

"Get me some water," said Alice turning to look at me.

"What do we say when we want something?" I said.

Her brow wrinkled and her eyes narrowed. "If you don't want to, just say so."

"OK. Ok…" I waved her off before I got yelled at. What's the use? I'm whipped and I know it. I set the coconut and the fruit down on the log and when to the bucket we kept in a nest of bushes to keep it out of the sun. It couldn't stay cool but it wouldn't be too warm either.

We'd managed to find a lime green plastic bucket from the boat that washed up on the beach a few days after the storm. Wreckage had washed up almost every day for the next two weeks after were stranded here.

We filled the bucket each morning with fresh water from a creek we found. The creek was close to the steep cliffs that guarded the lone mountain at the center of the island.

We had decided to keep our camp close to the beach and ferry the water from the creek because we didn't want chance missing any rescue boats or planes that might be looking for us. About as likely a possibility as my suddenly looking like Mr. Universe.

I picked up one of our three makeshift coconut drinking cups and filled it from the bucket. Once the coconut meat was removed it made a perfectly serviceable cup.

Alice didn't look up as I handed her the cup and sat down between them again. I began to work on my fruit. The sweet mango added much needed moisture to my mouth. Alice sipped at the water.

"There are caves nearby," said Val breaking the silence. "Near the cliffs. I saw them the other day when I was walking near there."

I nodded. "Yeah, Alice. Caves. We can take shelter in them."

Alice shot a look of indignation at me. "Why do you always have to agree with her?"

Val's face looked suddenly redder.

She picked up a branch from the pile of kindling we'd accumulated and like Alice started to poke away at a log in the fire. The wood crackled and flames leapt skyward.

I got up. This was ridiculous. We could handle this. We should handle this. Like adults. What we'd been doing up to now was acting like teenagers with petty jealousies.

I walked to the edge of the fire's circle of light then turned to face the two warring parties. They sat as far from each other as possible without falling off the end of the log.

"Listen, ladies. I know a little something about conflict resolution through negotiation, it's a technique called —"

"Oh, not that crap again," said Alice rolling her eyes heavenward. "He's always going on about this junk. He calls it the healing circle. Well, let me tell you something, sweetheart, it doesn't work, especially in this situation." She pointed an accusatory finger at Val.

Alice stopped speaking, her jaw was set in a determined line and her eyes were moist but scowled at me.

Val's eyes too burned with anger. She tossed the stick to the ground and whirled on the log to face Alice.

"I've listened to just about all I want to from you, Alice. I thought we'd all become friends, then a few days ago you seemed to think your husband and I...well, it doesn't matter what you thought. You're just wrong that's all. I'm not who you seem to think I am, and frankly I resent your insinuations."

With that Val stood and disappeared into the darkness headed in the direction of the beach. The night black as ink since there was no moon tonight. I could feel the breeze pick up an increase in wind speed suddenly brushed my cheeks. The wind pressed greasy hair flat against my forehead

The air smelled of ozone so I knew a storm was coming. A big storm like the one that stranded us here.

So not good.

\*\*\*

Sure enough the wind had turned into a howling gale by dawn. Rain the size of small cats pelted us as Alice and I huddled side-by-side under the wooden lean-to our hands wrapped around our knees. When we were younger we would have been hugging each other but the tension had evaporated those urges. But Alice refused to go to the caves and I was determined to support her.

Regardless none of this helped.

The palm fronds we'd used to construct the roof were quickly swept away by the high winds. The surf pounded the beach with a deafening roar. Bits of sand filled our mouths our eyes and our throats. It seemed like the end of the world.

"Where's your girlfriend?" said Alice in my left ear, her lips within inches of me. The raindrops stung my exposed areas of flesh and sheets of rain that came from the thick, black clouds overhead blurred my eyes. The air was occasionally split by peels of thunder and bolts of brilliant white and gold lightning lighted up the midnight clouds making them glow.

"She's not my girlfriend," I said, exasperated by her unrelenting attitude.

Alice sighed heavily and her shoulders drooped. "Yeah. I suspected as much."

Didn't she understand I loved her? I made one tiny mistake and it was over?

My eyes swept the deserted beach. It was covered with white foam due to the towering black waves of immense size and ferocity of the waves that rolled in over the reefs. The once calm lagoon had become a steaming chaos. "And before you ask. I don't know where she went."

Alice looked into my eyes and I saw the hard edge evaporate in her eyes.

We grabbed each and hugged tightly as if we never wanted to be apart ever again. We hadn't been this close in a long time and it felt good. If we died now I do so as a happy man. We broke our hug and she pressed her lips to mine. I kissed her back my heart pounding hard in my chest. We were like newly weds again.

***

By afternoon the rain had been reduced to slanted sprinkles of warm tap water and the wind had blown itself into a gentle breeze. We shivered in our wet clothes as we huddled under our re-built lean-to.

I decided I better find out what happened to Val. I hoped she hadn't been swept out to sea. If that were the case no one would ever find her body.

I stood and brushed the clingy sand off my body as best I could, then ran my hand over the scraggy, gray beard I had grown these past weeks.

"You stay here, Alice," I said, my voice low surprising even me with its intensity.

Alice gave a dubious look, but I knew she was tired and wanted to enjoy a nap now the weather had improved somewhat. She nodded and her mouth formed a gentle smile. She then laid her dirty blonde hair on her folded arms and closed her eyes. I knew she'd be in dreamland in no time.

As I left the lean-to I looked up at the forest-covered mountainside disappearing into the boiling clouds. The mountain peak was normally visible on clear days was obscured by the ink black clouds surrounding the peak. I'd taken to thinking of this silent monolith as ours. I shook my head.

What the hell was I thinking? We're not Tarzan and Jane.

Val had said there were caves at the base of the cliffs, and that those caves might be a better place to hole up than here on the beach. Given what Alice and I had just experienced I was thinking she might be right. Maybe Val had taken her own advice and was right now holed up in one of them waiting out the storm.

I didn't recall seeing any caves in our treks inland but they could certainly be there.

We'd salvaged some rope from the shipwreck, which I used to strap palm leaves to my feet to protect them from the sharp volcanic rocks strewn throughout the forest. It was a technique we'd learned on our early days on forays for food and water. The broad leaf palm leaves were tough and made excellent insulation.

I then started into the woods and was soon out of sight of the beach. As I trudged through the thick undergrowth birds called to each other in the trees overhead.

I sniffed the air and thought I detect the scent of smoke in the air. It was very faint, and came from my left. It was likely due to a lighting strike that had ignited some of the forest. The hard rains of earlier today would have quickly doused the flames, however, this afternoon I wasn't so sure.

Good thing the smell was so faint or I'd be more concerned. I would hate to be stuck on the beach if the weather all of a sudden turned worse again. Tropical storms were tricky things to predict.

After several exhausting minutes I stopped to sit on a fallen tree. My back hurt, my feet hurt, and my neck hurt.

"There you are," said a whispered voice from behind me. I whirled around on the log. Nothing. Maybe I was hearing things —

"Hello, Rob," whispered the sultry voice.

I turned my head quickly immediately regretting the sudden jarring of my already sore neck. The sight of Val in all her barely clothed glory rewarded my pain. Her eyes glowed with an inner light that made me sweat. My mouth dried and licked my lips.

"Val, I've been looking for you —"

"And I for you," she breathed making my heart beat harder against my rib cage.

She came toward me slowly at first then faster. She moved quicker than anyone I've ever seen until she stood over me her glowing eyes gazing down at me where I was seated on the tree trunk rubbing my sore feet.

"Listen, Val, there's some junk we need to clear up between us and Alice. I mean com'on there's no us now is there? One time doesn't count."

Val paused and her eyes fixed on mine. My stomach jumped with fear. There was something different about her eyes. I felt a chill run through my soul.

"You seriously think that was sex." She laughed harshly at my puzzled expression. "What nonsense. I bit you. I didn't mean to, but it's too late now. Its not something you can exactly take back you know."

"What….?" I felt the blood drain from my face. Bit me? What is she talking about? "I may be a 'wham bam thank you ma'am kind of guy, but I'm definitely not into the kinky stuff. I thought we had sex. In fact I'm pretty sure…." I paused. Hold on. Was my memory playing tricks on me? "...maybe not."

Val smiled and as she did I noticed her canine teeth were longer than the rest of her perfect white teeth. Val has model teeth. The kind Madison Avenue likes for TV toothpaste commercials.

I stared at her teeth and she snapped her mouth shut.

"I'm sorry, Rob. I should have told you two the truth about me."

I nodded. "I know you have a medical condition that requires measured doses of a drug I've never heard of. But since I'm not a medical doctor what do I know about it. The drug controls powerful urg…" My words trailed off as the revelation struck me as if I'd just been struck by lightning. "You're a vampire? Com'on. It's absurd. There are no such things. Vampires are a myth."

"Actually it's not a myth. There are people with rare blood disorders that cause them to have the urge to drink blood. My line has a genetic abnormally we control with drugs. My family became wealthy when we cornered the market on the drug and began to produce it in sufficient quantities."

I shook my head. "I still don't get it. What happens if you don't take the drug?"

"Then we become what fiction and the movies would call a vampire." She moved away her head bowed. "Many of my ancestors were hunted down and murdered because of this affliction. The drug makes it possible for us to live normal, productive lives."

"But you're able to walk around in the day. How is that possible?"

She laughed and my heart skipped a beat as I caught her heady scent. My hormones were on fire from the sound of her husky voice. "If you're referring to that nonsense about sunlight killing us, crosses and holy water, and sleeping in coffins filled with dirt, that's all utter nonsense. Hollywood fantasy. We're not the un-dead." She made those little quotation marks in the air with her long fingers.

"Oh," I said. What more can I say. This was far removed from my experience. "So what do we do now? I mean your drug is obviously gone."

"We feed our addiction of course."

Have you ever had one of those moments in life where things got creepy very fast? The skin on my arms was suddenly covered in goose bumps. This was one of those moments.

"What do you mean we?"

She shook her head. "I bit you. Isn't it obvious?"

"I'm infected…." The shock of that realization hit me like a freight train, which in the end would've been kinder.

"I spiked the water with the drug which is why I ran short. Now let's get Alice. We can share." Val turned to walk off and that's when I did it. I picked up a tree branch that had been blown down in the storm and rushed at her from behind.

I'm certain she didn't know what hit her as the tapered end of the length of branch impaled her. She dropped and fell on her face to the rich soil of the forest floor with a thump and lay still. Blood drained from around the entry point for several moments until it stopped to form a pool around Val's body.

I looked down at my blood soaked hands and couldn't believe what I'd just done. I didn't think I was capable of committing murder, but as I gazed down at Val's corpse I realized that somehow my physical strength had been multiplied.

One thing about vampires was true, a stake through the heart killed them. Then again being impaled with a stake can also kill regular humans. I killed someone. I killed Val.

I felt a rush of adrenalin as I made my way back to camp. The storm had abated completely by now and the heated tropical sun had managed to cut through the cloud cover causing mists of white steam to form all around me as I hurried my heart pounding in my chest.

I stepped out onto the beach to find Alice wasn't alone. A group of men surrounded her. They were dressed in navy uniforms. The bow of a gleaming white launch was partially dug into the sand.

Rescue. My heart began to race. We'd been rescued!

I stopped and froze where I stood. I thought of Val lying dead back in the woods and of the vampirism she'd infected me with. There were no drugs. I'd kill again. Next time it might be Alice. Next time the person might be an innocent.

I'm no murderer. I must confess. If they lock me up then everyone will be safe.

\*\*\*

I sit here on death row in my ten by six foot cell at the Texas State penitentiary awaiting my execution. Val's family has provided me with the drugs I need until my life will be ended. It's not so bad. It'll all be over soon.

Death isn't such a strange bedfellow. It's certainly preferable to life as a vampire.

Strange as it may seem Alice and I are closer now than ever in our twenty-five years of marriage. I told her I killed Val to stop her from harming her. I told her I did it for love. She said she understood.

At least someone understands.

# The Incredible Mr. Fix-It

HANK MUELLER STARED AT MRS. JONES toaster through his dirt specked, wire-rimmed reading glasses perched at the tip of his hawk-like nose. His white bushy eyebrows were arched on his forehead above pale gray eyes. The toaster rested on the counter of his fix-it workshop bench in the reception area at the front of the shop facing the window overlooking the quite street. A gray haired matronly woman stood on the other side of the counter watching him study her toaster in rapt attention, her watery eyes wide with expectation.

He eyed the switching mechanism closely as if he were a scientist gazing at a cold germ under a microscope. "Yes, he muttered to himself, "that must be…"

His heavily lined face cracked like a desert in the middle of summer when he broke into a wide grin. Mrs. Jones, the retired schoolteacher, one of his longest customers, smiled at him.

Her eyes glowed with pleasure about his assessment. Her ruddy moon-shaped face beamed with joy. Her grass green eyes focused on his looking back at her.

"I'll have this ready ta go in ten minutes. I have the parts in the back," Hank assured her.

The rear storage area of the modest fix-it shop occupied most of the one story brick building near the county's only auto wrecker yard. Inside the dank storage area were stacks of sand colored moldy cardboard boxes, carefully stored and catalogued, sitting on steel shelves. Each one was filled to bursting with machine parts of all sizes and shapes scavenged by Hank over the past fifty years.

Hank had little formal education, but he'd been a tinker all his life. He could fix anything. When he was three years old, he'd removed every cupboard door in his mother's kitchen with a Phillips screwdriver. His mother was horrified, but his father, who adored his only child, laughed and had taken it upon himself to encourage his son's natural ability to tinker.

His father was a gas fitter whose greatest joy in life were the weekly swap meets.

Young Hank had often accompanied his father into the forays into the world of pink flamingos, toys, games, musty books, carved home made wood signs, carefully lacquered and engraved with a family name like Smith, or Johnson, and every do-dad and odds and sods known to man.

Hank cherished the memory of these father and son outings. The treasures he and his father rescued from obscurity quickly became a shared obsession. Monstrously large steel framed calculators, with large plastic coated steel handles and ivory colored bulky plastic buttons that made a ratcheting sound when you pulled the handle. Engines for lawn mowers, model airplane parts, and unidentifiable electrical parts, from machines too foreign for them to identify. All these came home with them on many of these trips.

Hank would spend hours in the basement of his parent's home in the workshop deconstructing these strange objects. After these weird and wonderful machines were lovingly taken apart, Hank analyzed them and studied them to find out how they worked. He also learned by experimentation to fix them if they were broken. At first, he was able to make some work as they were supposed to, while others stumped him completely. This frustration made him work ever harder. He ached to know how things worked.

As the years went by, Hank collected more and more machines. His amassed collection soon comprised all types and sizes of devices, for every conceivable purpose known or unknown. Some didn't work when they first came home, not that this bothered Hank. He made them work. He fixed them.

As he passed through adolescence to manhood he discovered he was able to not only fix mechanical and electrical machines of all types, but in some cases he could make them better than their builders originally designed them. This became his true gift.

Hank left high school at the end of grade eleven bored by the structure and the lack of challenge inherent in formal education. He was determined to go his own way.

All through high school, Hank accepted odd jobs to fix people's machines. Teachers, housewives, his buddies, all types of people brought their bicycles, home appliances, lawn mowers, and in some cases, their cars, for Hank to fix. A few of the garages in town offered him jobs. He turned them all down preferring to accept small payments for helping his friends and neighbors.

After high school with the money he saved from these odd jobs, he bought the little abandoned auto parts shop near the wreckers yard and set up his tinker shop. He hung out a sign and became known around the county as the Incredible Mr. Fix-It, the guy who could fix anything.

Today, fifty years later, he was repairing Mrs. Jones toaster.

He shuffled into the back and studied the rows of boxes sitting on the blue steel shelves. On the top shelf, the fourth one from the bottom, he spotted the words, in his scrawled handwriting that read toaster parts. The musty smell of fifty years of accumulated dust that permeated the room didn't bother him.

He went to the corner of the room where he kept a stainless steel framed kitchen chair with a torn red vinyl seat. He hefted it and carried it the shelf where he'd found the parts he needed. Hank stood on the chair and gazed into the box. After rummaging through the oily parts, he found the switch for the same make, but the model one above Mrs. Jones' toaster, and stepped down. His worn, brown leatherwork boots squeaked in the silence of the room. He wiped his oily hands on the front of his stained, dark green coveralls.

He moved over to the wooden workbench against the opposite wall and turned on the spot light he kept attached to the bench. It was attached to a swivel assembly so pulled it toward him as he focused the yellow spot of light on the faulty switch. He pulled the proper size and type of screwdriver from the neat row of screwdrivers attached to a corkboard affixed to the wall in front of him over the bench. He removed the switch from the toaster with one deft turn of the screws then, after studying the replacement switch, and the now empty space where the old switch had been, saw that they were incompatible in size and shape.

No problem, he thought.

After ten minutes, exactly as promised, he reappeared behind the service counter to a startled Mrs. Jones who sat patiently in a chair in her navy blue, ankle length dress staring out the front window at the light rain falling across the cracked two lane paved road outside. Potholes peppered the old access road it had definitely seen better days. Hank liked to say it was as old as he looked.

"Here, Mrs. Jones," Hank said with a wide smile on his grizzled stubble covered features. His wispy white hair flew about his balding tanned head like shredded cotton in a mix master.

Mrs. Jones studied the toaster and saw the shiny new switch assembly. Somehow, it didn't look the same.

Seeing her puzzled expression Hank said, "I made it better. It'll never break again. The heating element'll last another year, but it's not worth fixing. You'll be gettin' a newin' then."

She nodded as she placed her glossy black vinyl purse on the finger print covered glass of the counter top. She pushed the gold colored latch and the purse clicked open.

"How much –" she started to say.

"Ten," he said.

She smiled warmly. She reached into the spot where she kept her household money in a side pocket, retrieved the proper bill, and placed it flat on the counter. "Mr. Jones will be so pleased. He loves his toast in the morning."

Hank nodded and picked up the ten, folded it in half then stuffed it in the left pocket of his coveralls. His customers were always saying much the same thing when he fixed their appliances, but after fifty years in the tinker business, he was becoming bored. Maybe it was time to retire.

He waved to Mrs. Jones as she bustled out the front door causing the little bell that hung off a hook over the door to chime brightly. But, he knew his ability to make people happy was the real reward for him; it was the one thing that made his life worth living.

He sighed and walked slowly into the back. He sat in the chair in front of the workbench and stared at the neat rows of screwdrivers, wrenches and other tools of his trade.

The bell over the front door interrupted his thoughts. Someone had entered the shop.

Accompanied by a creak from his knees he managed to lift himself from the chair and shuffled to the front. Two men greeted him as he entered the area behind the counter.

They were young men, the older of the two probably no more than thirty-five, the other considerably younger. The older of the two had his uniformed peaked cap tucked under his left arm. He wore a blue uniform, which meant he was in the Air Force. Hank didn't know much about the military ranks but he could tell by the expression of the other man, a blond crew cut made him look far younger than his real age, as he eyed the other man, the one smiling warmly and holding out his hand in greeting, was the more senior of the two.

His dark eyes and his dark brown crew cut made him appear like the serious military man he no doubt was.

These guys were so damned serious about every little thing, mused Hank. With their fancy razor pressed blue uniforms, spit polished brass buttons, colorful ribbons over the left breast pocket of their uniform jackets, and the gold wings over the right. They made quite a show of their superiority over lowly civilians like him.

Hank took the offered hand and smiled thinly. "Yes. How can I help you?" he said. Letting go of the air force man's hand, he buried both hands in the pockets of his coveralls. The man dark eyes flinched a little, but the smile stayed fixed to his tanned face, as he rubbed his now oily hand down his right pant leg.

"Mr. Mueller? I'm —"

"It's Hank and I gave at the office," said Hank.

The younger man looked around seemingly unsure what Hank meant. The older of the two chuckled uneasily.

"We're not here to collect for the old pilots retirement fund if that's what you think —"

"Actually, I thought it was tickets for the air force ball. You guys 'ave one don' ya, like firemen?"

The younger man frowned as it suddenly dawned on him that Hank was pulling their collective legs.

The older man's features shifted to a tolerant smile. His eyes said he wasn't amused with Hank's attitude. "Mr. Mueller, I think we're getting off on the wrong foot. My name's Major John Kenyon," Kenyon said as he indicated the younger man standing next to him. "This is Sergeant Williams. We're here to ask you for a favor."

Hanks senses were tweaked by the Major's revelation. The air force needed my help? An old tinker from a backwater county? He thought maybe he'd better give a listen might be interesting.

"You guys want some coffee?" Before they could respond, Hank was in the back room getting his raincoat. It was dirty yellow having been in his shops workroom for over thirty years. It was lined for warmth, but the heavy yellow plastic coated exterior was stained with oil and grease. He slipped his left arm in the sleeve as he walked to the front door.

"You comin'?" he said as he held the door open for the two air force men. The bell tingled in the silence of the room. Outside the rain had begun to fall harder.

The sound of the heavy raindrops hitting the gravel parking area along the road came clearly through the open door. The air was filled with the scent of wood smoke from the auto wreckers next door. Billy was again burning wood, reclaimed from the ancient cedars that ran along both sides of the road, to keep him warm in the guard shack.

The two men looked at each other uncertain if they should follow then the major shrugged and motioned for his subordinate to go ahead of him.

The sergeant placed his peaked cap on his wide square head and went into the rain. The major followed close behind. Hank smiled turned the button lock to secure the door behind them. He paused to turn the white plastic sign that hung off a hook secured to the door with a clear rubberized suction cup, in order that anyone seeing it would know he was closed.

Hank shook his head and smiled as he went outside and led them to the coffee shop not a block away. It was old one story stucco building, constructed in the same era as his tinker shop, with a half lit sign out front, the owner hadn't replaced the burned out fluorescent tubes inside the sign for the past three years. The place was called, as many similar greasy spoons across the country were, Mom's Diner.

By the time they were in the front door, and wiped their wet shoes on the dirty mat just inside the glass wood framed door, the military men's uniforms were a considerably darker blue, having been thoroughly soaked through by the rain.

The sergeant looked uncomfortably at the major who shrugged as they removed their caps and shook off the rainwater as best they could.

Hank led them to a booth by one of the large picture windows that overlooked the road. The interior was warm and dry and filled with the odor of freshly brewed coffee and homemade vegetable soup.

The waitress, a red haired woman of about forty, her white nametag identified her as Hazel, approached them. In her red finger nailed right hand she held a green and white order pad and her light pink waitress uniform was pressed and crisp. A bleached white apron tied at the back like a Christmas package covered the front of the knee length pink skirt.

She smiled as she approached, her heavy makeup seeming to crack as she exaggerated her hip swinging, as she spotted the two uniformed men. Her painted red lips, that surrounded pure white teeth, were turned upward at the corners.

"Hey, Hank how's it hanging?" she said her voice as cheerful as her smile.

"Good, Haze. Three coffees, okay?" he said pointing at the two men who sat shivering in their damp blue uniforms.

"Thanks, Mr. Mueller," said Kenyon. The sergeant nodded eagerly in agreement. Hank smiled thinly his gray eyes sparkling with amusement.

"I gather you boys need me," said Hank as Hazel dropped three full coffee cups in front of them along with plastic covered menus, one for each of them.

Kenyon took a sip of the warm, black coffee. His complexion became flushed again as the heat inside the diner penetrated his wet exterior. He shrugged. "Yes, sir…huh, sorry, Hank. Yes, we need your special talents."

"How do you know I have special talents?" said Hank his forehead wrinkled.

Sergeant Williams unbuttoned one of his breast pockets and pulled out a brown leather bound notebook, which he flipped, open.

"Hank Mueller, born August 22, 1936 to parents Kurt and Gertrude Mueller. The Mueller's emigrated to the U.S. in 1935 to escape the rise to power of Adolph Hitler. Kurt Mueller was a gas fitter until he died in a mysterious explosion in 1967. Mother, Gertrude Miller, died five years later of natural causes." Williams paused to flip the page.

"Hank Mueller left school at the end of grade eleven to start his own tinker shop, which he has owned and operated ever since." Williams finished, and with a flourish that would've rivaled the great swordsmen of Europe, he closed the notebook.

Hank eyed them closely as if he were studying them. Finally, he said, "You guys are pretty thorough. So what about me interests you?"

"We also hear you can repair anything and I mean anything. Some say you're a magician with machines," said Kenyon. He shrugged. "Of course, you're not a magician, but you're handy with machines and that is a talent that we need. Er, which your government needs."

Hank snorted and raised his cup to his lips his twinkling eyes peering at the two military men over the cups rim. "Why should I help you? Besides, don't you guys have your own mechanics and engineers to fix things? Where are your big brains when you need 'em?"

"Huh, it's kind of complicated," said Kenyon. His cheeks flushed crimson, but this time not due to the warmth of the room.

"What you got a broken toaster, or maybe a microwave that's makin' the boys in the mess glow after dark?"

Hank saw the sergeants eyes flit at the major who cringed as Hank rattled the man's cage. But Hank just couldn't help himself. He hated government with all their paperwork and miles of red tape. All his life he'd done everything he could to avoid contact with them. Now here they were on his doorstep asking for his help. How ironic was that?

Hank didn't have kids, or a wife, so he pretty much kept to himself. He had a pretty good life going. True the challenges had been rare these past few years, but why spoil all that by getting involved with these government geeks?

Hank leaned forward his expression serious. "Listen, unless you guys tell me what you want right now I'm gonna pack my kit and head back to my shop."

"Mr. Mueller, there's no need to…" said Kenyon.

"Now, or I walk," Hank said simply giving the two men a stern glare then shrugged and began to slide out of the booth. The cushion beneath him squeaked as he slid across its smooth surface.

Kenyon raised his hand to stop him and the sergeant stared wild-eyed at the senior officer. Hank's curiosity got the better of him and he stopped at the edge of the seat cushion.

"Okay, Mr. Mueller.." Hank gave the man a withering look. "Sorry. Hank," said Kenyon, though he looked uncomfortable being so familiar with a civilian. "We have a job for you at the base. A contract really. Short term. You don't have to enlist or anything if that's what you're thinking…"

Hank snorted.

Kenyon continued. "It's a thing…we're stumped…oh hell." Kenyon appeared lost for words.

The young sergeant, after glancing around to make sure no one was listening, spoke his voice low. "Mr. Mueller, it's an object from outer space. Unlike anything we've ever encountered and we need your help. We've tried everything to make it work. I'm the best tinker in the air force and even I can't make it operate."

"Did you try kicking it?" said Hank sarcastically.

The sergeant looked perplexed by Hank's suggestion. "Huh, no actually. Do you think that'll work?" Hank had to give the boy credit he had a heap o' enthusiasm.

Hank chuckled as he slid back to sit across from the two men. "Naw, boy. I was funin' with ya. How's about we go over to the base and you show me this thing whatever it is."

They nodded with Kenyon looking none too pleased.

Hank smiled as he lifted his cup and drained the remainder o the lukewarm coffee. The sergeant looked pleased with himself until the major cast him a disparaging look.

\*\*\*

An hour later, they pulled up in the regulation plain dark blue air force sedan in front of a dark abandoned hangar. Hank thought it was a Ford though it had no markings, except official ones, anywhere on the car.

The air base looked deserted for the most part, tumble weeds rolled by them and the wind carried the musty smelling desert into their nostrils through the open windows of the car. They stopped in front of the crescent shaped structure that towered upwards of five stories over their heads. Sure a biggin, thought Hank eyeing the large, dark structure.

As they stopped two figures dressed in dark green fatigues that made them near invisible each carrying an automatic rifle pointed directly at them, bracketed the car. Hank didn't know where they'd come from.

He'd not seen them as they pulled up until this very moment.

One stood in front of the car his rifle pointed at them while the other edged toward the drivers side of the car. The man in front's dark eyes scanned them, as did the barrel of his rifle, as if his hard eyes were sighting them like prey for the kill. A shiver of nervousness travel through Hank and then it was gone. He was with the two air force men. He didn't have anything to worry about. He hoped.

The second man shouldered his rifle, with a strap that was attached to the stock, and moved to the open drivers window.

Silently Kenyon handed the man a small black wallet. The man studied Kenyon's identification then held it up to check the picture against the real Kenyon. Satisfied he handed it back to the Kenyon.

"Major, I need Identification for the other two, sir."

The sergeant handed an identical black wallet to Kenyon who handed it to the grim faced guard. Hank, realizing he didn't have a little black wallet, pulled out his worn brown leather wallet from his coveralls back pocket and looked through it.

He smiled and nodded when he found what he was looking for and handed it to Kenyon who, without looking at it, handed the white plastic coated card to the guard. The guard leaned over and checked the sergeant against the picture in his wallet then gazed at Hank's id.

He handed it back to the major. "Not funny, sir." Kenyon looked at the card with a smiling picture of Hank. It was his library card that expired in 1972. Hank's hair was dark back then and covered his whole head.

"I'll vouch for him, airman."

The stone-faced airman stood back at attention then saluted. "Yes, sir." The airman nodded to his companion who lowered his rifle and with a blur of speed, they were gone. Hank couldn't see where they went. These guys were like ghosts, Houdini's, or something.

They stepped out of the car to stand in front of a black steel door. Hank didn't recall ever seeing pictures of hangars with doors like this one. It was massive and reminded him of his boyhood depictions of what the door at Fort Knox must look like.

They walked up to the door and Hank saw a stream of red light appear in front of them, which they would have to walk through to go any further.

Major Kenyon and Sergeant Williams walked through the light and with a groan of stressed metal against metal; the door began to slowly open outward. Hank hesitated watching the door begin to open. It was so damn big, he thought.

Kenyon stopped and looked back a small smile on his lips. "It's okay, Hank. The beam is a harmless low intensity-scanning device. It's perfectly safe."

Hank nodded then walked through the beam of light into the doorway created by the now open door.

Inside was a large bright room with a polished cement floor that gleamed. Hank stopped to glanced upward and saw the bare black walls that seemed to stretch forever over their heads until high above he saw the latticework of steel girders that made up the ceiling. Ahead of them was a raised platform with a tan colored service desk behind which sat two uniformed women watching them intently, their expressions hard. They wore camouflage fatigues similar to the men they'd encountered outside.

When they saw the new arrivals they stood and their hard blue eyes followed them as they crossed the open space between them. Hank could see they each had one hand resting on the butt of their pistols that hung off web belts obviously ready in case of trouble. These people are a little too paranoid, thought Hank.

The two women wore their hair up in ponytails. In black print over the right breast of their razor pressed camouflage shirts were their surnames. Norris and Lopez.

"Major," said Norris with a grim nod. Her icy expression focused on Hank. She didn't appear to appreciate civilian visitors.

"He's the IMFI," said Kenyon. Norris nodded at him her eyes expressionless. She stepped back and dropped her eyes to her seated companion. They exchanged a silent communication. What the hell was an IMFI? Hank thought for a moment then realized they meant him. Great, he thought, I've been reduced to an acronym.

At no time did she move to salute the major even though, as indicated by the two stripes on the collar of her uniform shirt, even Hank knew she was of a lower rank than either Kenyon or the sergeant. I thought they all had to salute superiors in the military.

"We're the repair team," said Kenyon.

Norris looked skeptical but she glanced at Lopez and nodded. The woman named Lopez reached beneath the counter, out of their line of sight, and flicked a hidden switch. A door appeared behind them and it slowly opened accompanied by the sound of compressed air escaping.

The two women then stood at attention eyes forward and saluted as Major Kenyon, Sergeant Williams, and a mildly amused Hank Mueller crossed the space to the open door. Kenyon and Williams returned the salutes as they headed away.

Hank suddenly realized that their footsteps should be echoing off these high walls yet there was only a slight rustling of their clothes as they moved. Something was absorbing the sound.

They entered through the door to find a lower more normal ceiling with a corridor containing a series of plain white doors than ran the length of the hallway. They seemed to stretch out for miles before them. The doors had no handles and the white tiles on the floor reflected their images as they walked. Mr. Clean must be their janitor, thought Hank. Again, there was no sound of their passage.

Kenyon stopped part way down the hallway. He reached into the right breast pocket of his uniform jacket to pull out a small sky blue card then slipped it into a barely discernible slit next to the door.

He smiled knowingly at Hank as the door slid aside into a recess in the doors frame. Hank nodded his pale gray eyes focused on the dark room they were about to enter.

"There's no turning back after we go in there," Kenyon said with a sideways glance at Williams who looked anxious.

Hank nodded silently. With all, this security whatever was in that room had to be something good and his natural curiosity, that had driven him most of his life, kicked in. He had to see it no matter what the consequences.

"Okay," said Kenyon. He reached inside the door and hit a button.

Large spotlights pierced the darkness focused on the center of the dark room where it lighted up a polished cement floor, like the one they'd seen in the other room. There, resting on a tri pod landing assembly was a ship or aircraft. Its appearance reminded Hank of a child's toy from a bygone era.

With a deliberate pace, Hank walked around the ship, which was itself round. It stood some ten to fifteen feet off the floor of the empty hangar. There were three, steel wheeled, red tool trays, each containing numerous drawers, standing off to one side as he passed on his way round the circumference of the vessel. It was obviously a space ship of some kind. An alien space ship. A big one.

A slow smile came over his face as he walked.

This was why they needed him, the Incredible Mr. Fix-It, the IMFI. He stopped in front of Kenyon and Williams with a wide grin fixed on his pale features.

"How much do you want to fix this?" said Kenyon.

Hank looked at them then at the ship. His eyes narrowed as he studied it and he rubbed his chin with his long narrow fingers in thought, finally, he said, "Nothing. I just want my chance at this baby."

Major Kenyon looked surprised while Williams beamed at him. Hank was beginning to take a shine to the little guy.

"Great," Williams said, "the NASA boys went to over this thing and over it again. They couldn't figure any of it out not even the basics. I was able to map the basic layout and…"

"That's okay, boy I'll make a tinker outta ya yet," Hank said as he placed one gnarled hand on the young man's shoulder to silence him. Hank couldn't help himself as he felt the enthusiasm emanating from this young man. It reminded him of him fifty years ago when he'd set up his shop. When the world was much younger.

"Why don't we get started," said Hank as he eyed Williams who stole a glance at Kenyon who shrugged his approval.

234

Kenyon then headed back out the door they'd entered through leaving the two men alone.

A ramp extended from the one section of the craft to the floor of the hangar. This would give them access to the interior. Williams walked toward the three tool stands.

" What do you need?" he said brightly.

Hank looked thoughtful then said, "I think a Phillips should do."

"Screw driver?" Hank nodded. "Anything else? We got everything.."

"Nope, just a Phillips. That's all."

Williams shrugged. "Okay, you're the boss." He reached into a drawer he'd opened and pulled out a long yellow handled screwdriver, of the size Hank suggested, which he handed to the older man. Hank took it and stuffed it in the back pocket of his coveralls.

"Say, boy what's your first name? I don't wanta be callin' ya Williams, or God help me sergeant, or some shit."

Williams smiled as he said, "Gabby, sir…"

"Hank. Please."

"Yes…Hank."

Hank slapped Gabby on the back and they laughed. They then walked up the ramp into the alien ship. It was time to get to work.

Gabby led Hank to the interior of the ship via doors that seemed to melt away as if they didn't exist as they moved through them. It was as if the ship were alive. The doors reappeared as they stood still in each room. The spacecraft contained four separate compartments with a central hub that joined them.

Gabby showed him the access hatch in the floor of one of he rooms where he'd discovered, when it was pulled back, what he speculated was the engine compartment. It wasn't very much larger than eighteen inches square. Hank studied the contents of the drive systems closely. He removed his wire-rimmed glasses and wiped them on one pant leg of his coveralls. It was the only spot on the soiled garment that wasn't covered in grease or oil. He then perched them back on the end of his long nose.

"Yes, he muttered, "that must be….."

Hank stood and turned to Gabby who scrambled to stand beside him. "Okay, you have to leave now."

"But…" stuttered Gabby, "I…"

Hank placed one hand on the young man's shoulder. "It'll be okay, Gabby. You just leave me and 'ol Betsy here alone for a spell and I'll have her up and runnin' for ya. OK?"

Gabby looked like he was going to hurt himself his face so twisted with his conflicting loyalties.

"I'll teach ya ta be a real honest to God tinker if ya let me," Hank said with a sly wink.

Gabby's features told Hank he'd won. The young sergeant resigned himself to letting Hank stay here by himself. What he couldn't hide was his disappointment at not being allowed to see how Hank worked his magic.

"One step at a time, boy," said Hank.

With his shoulders, slumped Gabby left the room through the door, which solidified once he was outside. Hank smiled to himself and pulled the screwdriver out of his back pocket. He hefted the weight of the long steel shaft with the heavy plastic handle in his hand then bent down to peer into the access bay.

\*\*\*

An hour later, he strolled down the ramp the screwdriver protruding from his back pocket. He had an oily handkerchief in his hands and was wiping them clean with it. He was also whistling softly to himself. The walls absorbed the sound of his out of tune whistle.

The door to the hangar burst open and Major Kenyon came rushing through followed by Gabby Williams. He stopped at the bottom of the ramp and watched Hank saunter down to meet them.

Hank's gray eyes were focused on his hands as he wiped them. He stopped in font of the two air force men.

"Well?" said Kenyon.

In response to his question, the ship began to hum softly and the metallic surface began to glow with an inner light.

"You've done it!" said Gabby, his voice that of a schoolboy on the last day of school before summer vacation.

Kenyon's eyes were wide as he stared dumbfounded at the alien ship suddenly come to life. His jaw hung open. "It can't be…" was all he managed to say.

"I'll see you boys later," said Hank with a small grin playing over his lined features. "I believe ma ride is sittin' outside?"

Gabby nodded and followed behind him like a puppy dog that smelled a treat coming.

When they were outside, and Hank seated in the back of air force car for the ride home, Gabby leaned toward car's passenger window. "You really are the Incredible Mr. Fix-It aren't you, Hank?"

"Yup," Hank said as he rolled up the window to separate them then the car drove off with another air force man at the wheel.

\*\*\*

Six weeks later Hank was busy in the back of his shop seated at the workbench peering at Mr. Wilson's broken lawn mover engine when the front door bell chimed signaling someone had just entered the shop.

He stepped to the front to find Major Kenyon standing at the counter. Gabby Williams was noticeably absent. Kenyon appeared upset and embarrassed.

"What can I do for ya, Major?" said Hank.

"We lost it," he said his voice barely above a whisper.

"Lost what?"

"IT." He lowered his voice. "You know it." Kenyon gave him a knowing look with dark eyebrows raised over watery red-rimmed eyes. Hank discerned from the rumpled condition of his uniform Kenyon must've slept in his, for more than one night. There had to be at last two days growth of black stubble adorning his chiseled jaw.

Hank shook his head in sympathy then said, "I guess you boys blew it, didn't ya?"

Kenyon's face became red and his eyes reflected a sudden burst of anger. "It took Williams with it," he said between gritted teeth

Hank's smile disappeared and he frowned. "Well, then that's very different. I guess I better get 'im back for ya."

"How're you going to do that?"

"They don't call me the Incredible Mr. Fix-it because it's a good advertising slogan ya know." Hank moved around the counter and put an arm across Kenyon's broad shoulders as he led him to the front door. He opened the door.

"You just run along to your base and leave everything to me. I find that young fella for ya."

The bewildered major gazed at the tinker and after straightening his tie, which was askew, he marched off to the nondescript blue air force car that sat waiting to take him back to the base.

Hank watched the car until it disappeared behind a stand of trees at the end of the road where it curved. He turned and sighed heavily. Poor Gabby, a victim of his own success. Now he had to get him back. He knew the aliens were gonna be none too pleased.

He closed the door, turned to sign around to the closed side, then walked into the storage room in the back of the tinker shop. He closed the door behind him with a thump.

He walked past the shelves piled high with boxes of law mower, toaster, microwave and television parts until he'd made his way to the far wall at the back. There against the wall were three steel shelving units filled with cardboard boxes stacked to the ceiling. The boxes were labeled 'SPACE SHIP PARTS'.

Hank stared at the mountain of boxes and shrugged. Might as well get started, the sooner I start the sooner it'll be done.

# The Legend of G and The Dragonettes

It's good to be the princess.

Cinnamon's thoughts were interrupted when the sixty-thousand unruly, unwashed peasants in the overflowing stadium, cheered the death of latest in a long and undistinguished list of pretenders for her hand in marriage. Far below the royal platform in the arena Val the Valiant has just lost his head upon the closing of the dragon's jaw

Cinnamon sighed. Another one bites the dust. Not much a hero if you ask me.

Princess Cinnamon glanced over her left shoulder at her beloved Dragonettes dressed in their red cheerleader uniforms and matching sneakers provided by their team sponsor, Castle Mart.

As team captain, these fresh faced girls were her pride and joy, her reason for living, except…why is there always an except?

Her intelligent indigo eyes settled on the latest in a long tradition of sworn enemies, Penny Trueheart.

Not that Penny knew she was the enemy. But such is the lot of the rival. It seemed every year someone in Cinnamon's cheerleader squad had at least one rivalry. This year it was her turn to have a rival and Penny was the rival du jour.

You're not getting my man, witc —

The smell of Val's blood wafted up and over the cheering crowd. Cinnamon was forced to cover her delicate ears as the crowd roared its approval. When sixty thousand spectators cheer you feel it as much as you hear it.

If only it had been Penny in the arena, now that would be something worth watching. But, Cinnamon had no time today to dream about the fate of Penny Trueheart. It was show time.

Her lips curled into her best look-at-me-I'm-so-pretty smile. Behind her stood the mostly hand picked squad, with the exception of Penny, who was chosen by Cinnamon's step-mother, Queen Pepper. Cinnamon was certain the Queen had picked Penny out of spite. As you'd expect her father sided with the Queen.

The Dragonettes included; the ultra-athletic Thyme, sweet but simple Rosemary, cute-as-a-button Sage, and the twins, Garlic and Onions (pronounced O-ny-uns by Garlic and Onions rather odd parents. Garlic on the other hand, while a pungent name, is pronounced in the usual way).

Cinnamon spun round to face her Dragonettes, her pom-pom's held high, her feet set apart in the perfect position, just as they had practiced, ready to deliver the new cheer Cinnamon had written and choreographed personally.

"What do we say, Dragonettes?!"

The well-drilled unit of teenage faces beamed with youthful pride. "The Dragonettes say; Go! Dragon Joe! Go!"

Cinnamon sprang off the ground her long, not too muscular legs folded underneath her as she became airborne. She unfurled her legs and landed once more on the heavy timbers that made up the deck. She landed with a soft thump. As leader Cinnamon shook her pom-poms to signal the next sequence.

The Dragonettes yelled with wild whoops and high spirits and shouts of "Go Team!" They leaped about in what looked to the uneducated like random chaos. Of course, Cinnamon was an expert in cheerleading.

Her late mother had taught her many of the finer points of cheerleading and was considered the expert in the kingdom.

The Dragonettes cheers stirred the crowd into a frenzy of blood lust. Men, women, and children rose to their feet to scream in unison, "Go, Joe! Go! Go! Go, Joe!"

Joe curled his long spiked tail and roared, his voice echoed over the crowd. As one they roared back. Joe then threw his head back and shot a river of flame high into the air. Even from the royal platform Cinnamon could feel the heat from Joe's fire.

The three hundred guards that ringed the arena had their crossbows trained on Joe in case he strayed from the script.

Cinnamon turned to face the crowd and shook her pom-poms at the audience. This caused even more wild jubilation and wild cheers to erupt. Pagania was going to be a wild kingdom tonight.

The dragon, one of those wingless wonders, with a razor sharp bone ridge that ran up the long snout, and green scales, that were the color of mold on month old bread, covered its lizard-like body, redirected the stream of molten fire over the torso that had once been attached to Val's head.

Upon contact Val's torso burst into flame, black smoke rolled outward to fill the stadium air. It overpowered the smell of Val's blood.

Cinnamon's spirit soared; the barbecued Val-the-not-so-Valiant would never become her betrothed.

Though I sure do love good barbecue, thought Cinnamon.

There would be no husband for her today. And no deflowering. The King's proclamation said that only a hero who defeated the dragon in combat had the right to claim her hand in marriage.

A barbaric rule if you ask me.

The crowd roared their approval as the hungry flames consumed the body of the late Val.

But celebration soon turned into disappointment that the end had arrived. The atmosphere of blood lust and excitement deflated as The Orator of the Games walked out from behind a wall to stand on the royal platform looking over the crowd. The platform was in front of the royal box, where her mother and father sat on their gilded thrones, and where Cinnamon and the Dragonettes performed their routines.

The Orator, rail thin Larry the Loud, dressed in his royal blue robe with the gold thread ankle length robe, held his arms out from his sides, palms down, to signal the crowd for silence.

His strong chin, with its close-cropped goatee, stuck out in the confident manner Larry always used when he performed before an audience. As one and according to an unwritten program the over stimulated crowd fell silent.

The oval shaped stadium was designed to relay the sounds in such a way that the Orator could be heard from every seat.

As Larry began to speak his baritone voice carried over the crowd. "Citizens of Pagania. Your great and glorious, King Salt has given you today the spectacle of the last challenger from the far off mysterious lands of the East. Today —"

Cinnamon tuned out the rest of Larry's speech, preferring instead to study the crowd. She felt a deep longing within her as she scanned the faces.

Surely somewhere in the world there had to be her hero, her champion. Not that she wanted a husband necessarily, but daddy would be so disappointed if she didn't some day produce an heir and a spare. Maybe she'd even find her true love. A man who loved her that she could truly love would certainly the icing on the cupcake.

A liberated woman living in the thirteenth century who finds true love is a not as common as you might think.

Even when she's a member of the thin and rich. Good thing daddy's loaded or I'd have to settle for a goat herder.

It's good to have a king for a daddy.

Cinnamon shifted her attention to the arena floor where the Dragon wranglers were herding the dragon out the massive blue steel doors located at the south end of the arena. To do these sixteen men used ten-foot long poles, tipped with jagged steel spikes. It was a wise man who said I wouldn't touch a dragon with a ten-foot pole.

The dragon wranglers were the very poor who needed a job. One man is always assigned as the wrangler jester. Wrangler jesters amused the crowd by taunting the dragon as it was being taken away.

Jokes on you if he gets mad.

But the dragon didn't seem interested in the jester or the sixteen herders. His head hung low, he looked tired.

The heavy steel doors clanged shut as they closed behind them. The dragon would be locked in a reinforced iron cage deep in the bowels of the stadium, far below the arena floor.

With the death of the last hero from the East Cinnamon knew it was decision time.

Larry and daddy had scoured the world to find her champion and so far they had failed to find the right man. Cinnamon decided she must take the dragon by the tail. It was time for action.

*** 

After she'd dismissed her team for the day Cinnamon made her way to the entry of the tunnels that ran in a spiral pattern beneath the ancient stone structure. No one knew when these tunnels had been built. Some said they were built by Alexander the Great.

The tunnels were humid and yet cool after the afternoon heat. The air was musty and stank of the centuries old build up of mold and mildew. Cinnamon wrinkled her perfect nose as made her way along the corridor. Torches burned bright and she could detect the scent of the oil used to keep them lit.

She had been given approval to visit the lower levels by the head dragon wrangler, a seedy character named Lupe.

Guys loopy all right.

There was a curve to the right in the wall ahead. She froze when she heard the heavy breathing for the first time.

Though she was warm enough her lean framed trembled.

She edged around the wall, her back against cool stone. Her cheerleader uniform would need a good cleaning after this but right now she didn't care.

There it was, the dragon lying on its belly in it's barred enclosure, its eye slits closed, its thick body rose and fell in time with its breathing. Fortunately for her the bars were thick and strong enough to prevent the massive creature from swallowing her without so much as a dash of seasoning.

"I'm not an it!"

Did I say that out loud? Hey, wait a minute… did it say something?

"I said, I'm not an it!"

It spoke! "What magic is this, dragon!" she said, her voice trembled, not with bravado but with absolute terror.

"Humans. Females. Cheerleaders! Bah! Go away, cheerleader," said the dragon in his growl-speak.

Very few people these days spoke dragon anymore, but she had taken a course on dead languages at the nunnery and was fluent. The old Nun who ran the place was an expert and an excellent instructor.

"Your name is Joe, is it not?" said Cinnamon regaining some measure of confidence.

"It is." The Dragon named Joe lifted his head. His black eyes stared at her. "I should kill you where you stand," he said in a matter of fact that sent a chill through her. His eyes narrowed.

She could smell the oil and brimstone coming from the dragon's mouth as he spoke.

"I have a proposition, Joe" she said.

"A deal?" said the Dragon.

"Yes."

"Well, out with it, cheerleader. I haven't got all day. And don't get so familiar. Dragon's hate to be taken lightly. I could just as easily smoke you where you stand."

"Places to go, people to see, huh? Is that it, Joe?" She knew she was pushing, but dragons were legendary for their love of the deal.

The dragon sat silent for several seconds. Cinnamon was sure he was about to breath fire and end her world when Joe spoke again. "Come closer." Cinnamon hesitated. "Oh, don't be silly. I'm not going to barbecue you!"

Cinnamon edged forward until she stood next the steel bars that separated them. The dragon's breath was horrid. It reeked of rotten meat and decay. She managed to hold her gag reflex in check.

"I was wondering if you know of any heroes. You know…strays…who my father may have missed."

The dragon looked thoughtful then he said, "Yes, I believe I know of one. He's from some place called Houston."

"Houston? Never heard of it."

"It's very far away. But I heard about him through the dragon network —"

"Dragon network? What's that?"

Joe's eyes narrowed. "Never interrupt a dragon when they're talking," he growled his voice edged with menace.

It felt weird enough to be talking to a dragon in the first place, but a rude dragon? That was another matter.

She'd scoffed at the old Nun when they told her she'd use the dragon's language some day, but now here one was scolding her. Cinnamon nodded. She needed this creatures help so heap on the abuse you big ugly lizard she could take it.

"Before we go on," said the dragon, "let's get something straight. I'm not a creature, or a dragon for that matter. My name is Joe. I'd prefer if we stick to first names. What's your name?"

"Uhhh…do you read minds?"

"What geniuses these humans be." The dragon rolled his eyes and snorted a small ball of fire. "All I'm asking is your name, girl."

"Cinnamon."

"Like the spice?"

"Uhhh…yeah…I guess so."

"And your friend's names are Thyme, Rosemary, Sage, Garlic and Onions?" He pronounced it Onions not O-ny-uns, but she wasn't about to correct him. "What are you the spice girls?"

"Uhhh…no…we're the Dragonettes."

Joe threw his massive head back and erupted in laughter sending chills through her.

*\*\*\**

Cinnamon left the tunnels behind feeling the best she had in weeks. The deal was done. Joe had agreed to help her become head cheerleader. In return she'd ensure he was freed from his present job. The dragon was pleased about his freedom after she ordered the guard to release him. The guard opened his mouth to protest until she reminded him she is the princess and must be obeyed under pain of death.

It's good to be the princess.

She rounded the corner at end of the path leading to the castle and nearly bumped into Penny. Penny bowed her head when she realized who it was she'd almost collided with. Cinnamon detected Penny's jasmine perfume and felt a twinge of jealousy.

*I probably reek of ode de dungeon.*

"Sorry, Princess," said the pretty, petite blue-eyed blonde.

"Ah, Penny just the…I was looking for." Penny lifted her gaze a puzzled look in her eyes. "I'm planning to meet a new suitor at the edge of the village when he arrives tomorrow."

Penny's pale eyebrows rose up her forehead. "Really, Princess? Another suitor? I thought —"

"As did I until I learned of another hero. A saintly man named G."

"G? Just G?"

"No, of course not. His full name's Sir George of Houston, but he prefers to go by G. I'm told all the popular crown heads go by single letters these days. And you know how fads are; here today, gone tomorrow." Cinnamon laughed. "In a month or two he may go by Eorge."

Penny looked thoroughly confused, but she nodded anyway.

"Meet me near the end of the road, where the last of the peasant cottages are, at noon to meet this new hero. I'll introduce you. Be precise. I hear this new hero is quite punctual." Penny nodded then went around Cinnamon and disappeared around the corner.

Soon, Penny Trueheart. Soon, thought Cinnamon as she watched her rival leave.

\*\*\*

Cinnamon arrived a few minutes early, which gave her time to check the thick bushes behind the row of shabby cottages. Sure enough, Joe was hidden there just as they'd agreed. Upon seeing her he gave her a wicked grin and winked. She shuddered.

I'm in league with the devil for sure. Good thing I'm a pagan.

Cinnamon left Joe in the bushes and walked back to stand beside the dirt road.

An old woman sat on a stool outside the last cottage. She seemed oddly familiar, but Cinnamon dismissed the thought. She was like any other peasant. Pathetic and poor. Between her dry lips the old woman clasped a corncob pipe. A trail of thin white smoke drifted into the air from the bowl. The woman studied Cinnamon from where she sat.

Cinnamon tried to ignore the woman's gaze by looking up and down the road.

"What ya up to, Princess?" said the woman.

"You know who I am?"

"Of course," said the woman with a glint in her dark eyes. "You're one of them Dragonettes." The scent of the smoke from her pipe was pleasant it had a sweet, nutty aroma.

Cinnamon nodded. It felt good to be recognized. She'd become a celebrity. Another dream realized.

""You made a deal with Joe, didn't ya?" said the old woman. She smiled.

"How did you know?"

"I did the same thing once. I speaks their language."

Cinnamon scoffed. She speaks dragon? I hardly think so. "What could an old woman like you gain from a deal with Joe the dragon?"

"True love. Same as you."

Cinnamon started. A chill ran up her spine. "And?"

The woman shrugged. "Turned out not too bad."

Cinnamon balled her hands on her hips. "I'm a princess. Things always turn out well for me." Cinnamon puffed out her chest and smiled.

"I'm the spoiled pagan princess."

The woman cackled, as old women are wont to do, then said, "Of course, Princess. Of course." She rose from her stool and disappeared through the cottage door.

Fine way for the old lady to talk. She'd put the old bag in her place. Cinnamon placed her right thumb on her chest. "I'm the princess around here. You think I've never made a deal with a dragon before?" Of course she hadn't, but the peasant woman didn't need to know that. "Well I have, old crone. You better believe it."

Penny soon appeared in the distance coming from the direction of the castle. Once outside the thatched house of the old crone she smiled shyly at Cinnamon, which made Cinnamon wince. Girl, you're as sweet as honey. And I hate honey.

Beyond the village, green fields lay as far as the eye could see. Against this backdrop he came. A young man, with long dark hair, broad shoulders and lean hips astride a magnificent pure white stallion. What a man, Cinnamon thought.

He wore a hat the color of new snow. It shape was unlike anything Cinnamon had ever seen. And his pure white pants, shirt, boots and saddle gave him the appearance of a white knight.

His features were equal parts rugged and sensitive. His face was tanned, with a dimple on his chin. His body looked toned but not too muscular.

Cinnamon felt a strong urge to fall into his arms. He could be the one.

The old woman sat on a nearby by tree stump watching puffing on her pipe. Cinnamon could have told her to leave, but the old lady might learn something about her princess today. Fear of your local monarchy was healthy and natural.

He rode up to the two women and reined his horse as he came to a stop in front of them. The horse was a magnificent stallion that stood still and calm as could be.

"Howdy, ma'am," he nodded and tipped the front brim of his hat with the strong fingers of his right hand. Cinnamon didn't know if all the men of this Kingdom of Houston were like him, but if G was a representative sample then Huston must be one beautiful realm.

Cinnamon and Penny curtsied together. "Good day, Sir G."

"Name's plain old George. Folks jus' call me G. My daddy's name is Big G."

"Is his name George too?" asked Penny. Cinnamon glared at her.

Penny looked embarrassed and averted her eyes from her leader's gaze.

"Yes, ma'am. George Senior is muh daddy's name."

"Ignore her, G," said Cinnamon. "I hope she hasn't given you the wrong impression. We don't usually ask such personal questions of strangers who come to our town for the first time."

G shook his head. "No worries, ma'am." He dismounted and stepped to the front of the horse the reins held in his right hand. "I understand thuh reason 'm here is ta slays a dragon and save a fair maiden. Is that right?"

Cinnamon nodded. "Yes, that's right."

"Well then ya'll lead me ta the arena. I gots some dragon blood ta spill."

"Actually you won't be fighting the dragon in the arena."

He frowned and she felt her go flutter. Soooo handsome. Maybe being a liberated woman in the thirteenth century wasn't all it was cracked up to be.

"Sorry, ma'am I don't rightly understand. The dragon needs ta be emulated…uhhh…I mean emasculated…I mean…"

Cinnamon couldn't hold back any more. She stepped toward G and threw her arms round his neck. G cried out in horror, ripped her arms from his neck, and pushed her away.

"What's the matter with ya'll? Women don't touch a man like that lessen they's married."

Cinnamon flushed with embarrassment, and a little anger, but she had no regret for having made her move. Secretly she had hoped to encourage him to go farther. But it appeared he was as old fashioned and stuffy as her father.

I hate rules.

Branches crunched from the row of thick bushes behind them, this was accompanied by a thump of heavy footsteps. Joe appeared from the bushes, his scales covered in leaves, stuck there by spider's webs that now surrounded his body in a loose cocoon of spider spit. "Never fear! Joe is here!" the dragon roared.

"The dragon!" cried G as he stepped to his white horse and withdrew a four-foot long sword from a scabbard attached to his saddle. The sword's polished blade gleamed in the sunlight.

The white cowboy knight brandished the sword using both of his strong hands to wrap round the hilt.

He moved with fluid and grace as he circled the dragon warily. Doubt crossed Joe's face. He glanced at Cinnamon who shrugged.

Joe cocked his head back and shot a stream of fire at the challenger. G tumbled across the grass until he once again stood on his feet the weapon again poised for battle. He wore an arrogant smirk on his handsome features. He had managed avoid the searing death-dealing flames far too easily.

As if on a cue Joe edged toward Penny who appeared to be mesmerized by the battle.

Cinnamon's lips curled in knowing smile. This was it. This would be the end of her rival. Set up. Too late for you, Penny.

The dragon whirled his massive body and his massive jaws closed over Cinnamon. Cinnamon emitted one weak cry of surprise and then she was gone.

\*\*\*

G lowered his sword to his side. With a grin on his ruddy face he sauntered walked toward Penny and wrapped his left arm around her trim waist.

"I thought she'd never leave," said Penny. She patted the old woman on the knee. Thank you, mother, for teaching me dragon speak and for helping me realize my dreams." The old woman said nothing but she wore a satisfied smile on her lips.

She turned to look at Joe. "And thank you, Joe."

The dragon shrugged. "A deals a deal." Joe cocked his head. "Are you going to be the new head cheerleader of the Dragonettes?"

Penny nodded then turned to face G whose handsome features broke into a wide smile.

"Be on your way. As agreed in our double double cross deal you're a free dragon," Penny said before she kissed G hard on the lips. The King would wonder what happened to one of his eighteen daughters, but everyone knew Cinnamon was far from his favorite. There were plenty more where she came from.

Joe disappeared into the rolling grass covered hills. He was never seen again. Penny Trueheart and G lived happily ever after.

And the Dragonettes? They won the regional finals and went on to become the national champions.

# About the Author

International selling author, Russ Crossley writes romance under the name R.G. Hart, mystery/suspense under the name R.G. Crossley, and science fiction and fantasy under his own. This year there will be re-issues the romantic comedies, Bachelorette: Zombie Edition by Champagne Books, and Antique Virgin by 53rd Street Publishing, paranormal romantic comedy, Zomopolis, and a new western romance entitled, The Fire In Their Hearts co-authored with R.S. Meger will be published in 2013 by Champagne Books. Also, look for another Aloha adventure, Bloody Betty Queen of the Pirates coming in the spring of 2013 from Champagne Books.

In addition the near future suspense novel, The Last Serial Killer by R.G. Crossley was recently released by 53rd Street Publishing in ebook and trade paperback versions.

He has sold several short stories that have appeared in anthologies from Pocket Books, St. Matins Press, at Smashwords, Amazon, and other e-retail sites.

With his wife, romance author R.S. Meger, he owns and operates a small press publishing company, 53rd Street Publishing. The company began in April 2011 and now has over one hundred e-book titles and a number of print titles, with more planned in 2012 and 2013.

He is a member of SF Canada and the Greater Vancouver Chapter of Romance Writers of America. He is also an alumni of the Oregon Coast Professional Fiction Writers Master Class taught by award winning author/editors, Kristine Katherine Rusch and Dean Wesley Smith.

To find a complete listing of his work check out his website http://www.rghart.com, http://russstory.blogspot.com.Razor's blog can be found at http://razorandedge.blogspot.com

Feel free to contact him on Facebook or Twitter. He loves to hear from readers

# Other books by the Author

Titles as R.G. Crossley

Short Stories

Razor and Edge Mysteries
The Kidnapping of Billy Buttons
String of Pearls
Death by Clown
Beggin' For Murder
Ragged Ice
The Grand Central Mystery
A Strange Case of Undead Murder

Non-Series Mysteries
A Day Without Sunshine
Mirror Image
Dangerous Waters
Cape Disappointment
Boomerang
The Watcher of Wayburn Street
The Apprentice
Drip!
A Beautiful Friendship and The Parrot of Doom
Robine's Diary
The Christmas Club
Loose Ends
Skullduggery
Splatter Pattern
It Takes Two

Anthologies
The Adventures of Razor and Edge:
Five Tales From The Quirky Detective Team

Novels
A Bad Case of Loyalty
The Last Serial Killer
Shear Murder

Titles as Russ Crossley

Novels
Attack of the Lushites

Short Stories
Countdown
Shoeless Moe
Round Up At The Burger Bar:
The Story of Trixie Pug, Parts 1, 2, 3, 4, 5, 6, 7
Five Minutes
Blossom Queen, Barbarian
The Secret
The Family Line
End of the Flies
With Death You Get the Eggroll
The Penguin Sleeps With The Fishes
Only The Worthy
Hero For A Day
End of Empire
Strange Bedfellows
Big Business
A Perfect Crime

The Wise Guy and The Pirates
In Search of the Perfect Cup
T.I.N. Men
The Legend of G and the Dragonettes
The Incredible Mr. Fix-It
Lock Stock and Barrel
Divided Loyalties
Cave of Wonders
A Family Empire
Until We Meet Again
Dragon Rising

Presents Anthology Series
Five Tales of Urban Fantasy
Five Tales of Bizarre Detectives
Five Tales of Mystery and Suspense
Five Tales of Weird Fantasy
Spies, Detectives, & Heroes
Tales of Twisted Crime
Five Tales of The Unexpected
Tales From Space
10 by Russ Crossley
Round Up At The Burger Bar: The Story of Trixie Pug,
Parts 1- 5 The Beginning
Worlds of Science Fiction and Fantasy
More Tales of Mystery and Suspense
Ladies of the Jolly Roger
Justice Served

Titles as R.G. Hart

Short Stories
Tikka's Big Day
"My Partner the Zombie" —
Hungry For Your Love Anthology
(St. Martin's Press)
Big Hairy Deal
One Red Shoe
A Bad Day in Lunden Texas
Hook Island
Grind Manor
Bloody Betty, Queen of the Pirates (coming soon from
Champagne Books)

Novels
Bachelorette: Zombie Edition
(from Champagne Books)
Antique Virgin
The Fire In Their Hearts
with R.S. Meger (coming soon from Champagne
Books)
Zomopolis